THE LAST WHITE MAN

Exclusive signed edition

Mohsin Hamid

August 2022

HAMISH HAMILTON
an imprint of
PENGUIN BOOKS

THE LAST
WHITE MAN

Mohsin Hamid

HAMISH HAMILTON
an imprint of
PENGUIN BOOKS

HAMISH HAMILTON

UK | USA | Canada | Ireland | Australia
India | New Zealand | South Africa

Hamish Hamilton is part of the Penguin Random House group of companies
whose addresses can be found at global.penguinrandomhouse.com.

First published in the United States of America by Riverhead Books,
an imprint of Penguin Random House LLC 2022
First published in Great Britain by Hamish Hamilton 2022
001

Printed and bound in Great Britain by Clays Ltd, Elcograf S.p.A.

The authorized representative in the EEA is Penguin Random House Ireland,
Morrison Chambers, 32 Nassau Street, Dublin D02 YH68

A CIP catalogue record for this book is available from the British Library

ISBN: 978–0–241–56657–2

www.greenpenguin.co.uk

Penguin Random House is committed to a
sustainable future for our business, our readers
and our planet. This book is made from Forest
Stewardship Council® certified paper.

For Becky

PART
ONE

One

One morning Anders, a white man, woke up to find he had turned a deep and undeniable brown. This dawned upon him gradually, and then suddenly, first as a sense as he reached for his phone that the early light was doing something strange to the color of his forearm, subsequently, and with a start, as a momentary conviction that there was somebody else in bed with him, male, darker, but this, terrifying though it was, was surely impossible, and he was reassured that the other moved as he moved, was in fact not a person, not a separate person, but was just him, Anders, causing a wave of relief, for if the idea that someone else was there was only imagined, then of course the notion that he had changed color was a trick too, an optical illusion, or a mental artifact, born in the slippery halfway place between dreams and wakefulness, except that by now he had his phone in his hands and he had reversed the camera, and he saw that the face looking back at him was not his at all.

Anders scrambled out of his bed and began to rush to his bathroom, but, calming himself, he forced his gait to slow, to become more deliberate, measured, and whether he did this to assert his control over the situation, to compel reality to return through sheer strength of mind, or because running would have frightened him more, made him forever into prey being pursued, he did not know.

The bathroom was shabbily but comfortingly familiar, the cracks in the tiles, the dirt in the grouting, the streak of dried toothpaste drip on the outside of the sink. The interior of the medicine cabinet was visible, the mirror door askew, and Anders raised his hand and swung his reflection into place before his eyes. It was not that of an Anders he recognized.

He was overtaken by emotion, not so much shock, or sorrow, though those things were there too, but above all the face replacing his filled him with anger, or rather, more than anger, an unexpected, murderous rage. He wanted to kill the colored man who confronted him here in his home, to extinguish the life animating this other's body, to leave nothing standing but himself, as he was before, and he slammed the side of his fist into the face, cracking it slightly, and causing the whole fitting, cabinet, mirror, and all, to skew, like a painting after an earthquake has passed.

Anders stood, the pain in his hand muted by the intensity that had seized him, and he felt himself trembling, a vibration so faint as barely to be perceptible, but then stronger, like a dangerous winter chill, like freezing outdoors, unsheltered, and it drove him back to his bed, and under his sheets, and he lay there for a long while, hiding, willing this day, just begun, please, please, not to begin.

Anders waited for an undoing, an undoing that did not come, and the hours passed, and he realized that he had been robbed, that he was the victim of a crime, the horror of which only grew, a crime that had taken everything from him, that had taken him from him, for how could he say he was Anders now, be Anders now, with this other man staring him down, on his phone, in the mirror, and he tried not to keep checking, but every so often he would check again, and see the theft again, and when he was not checking there was no escaping the sight of his arms and his hands, dark, moreover frightening, for while they were under his control, there was no guarantee they would remain so, and he did not know if the idea of being throttled, which kept popping into his head like a bad memory, was something he feared or what he most wanted to do.

He attempted, with no appetite, to eat a sandwich, to be calmer, steadier, and he told himself that it would be all right, although he was unconvinced. He wanted to believe that somehow he would change back, or be fixed, but already he doubted, and did not believe, and when he questioned whether it was entirely in his imagination, and tested this by taking a picture and placing it in a digital album, the algorithm that had, in the past, unfailingly suggested his name, so sure, so reliable, could not identify him.

Anders did not normally mind being alone, but as

he was just then, it was as if he was not alone, was, rather, in tense and hostile company, trapped indoors because he did not dare to step outside, and he went from his computer to his refrigerator to his bed to his sofa, moving on in his small space when he could not stand to remain a minute longer where he was, but there was no escaping Anders, for Anders, that day. The discomfort only followed.

He began, he could not help it, to investigate himself, the texture of the hair on his scalp, the stubble on his face, the grain of the skin on his hands, dry, the reduced visibility of the blood vessels there, the color of his toenails, the muscles of his calves, and, stripping, frantic, his penis, unremarkable in size and in heft, unremarkable except in not being his, and therefore bizarre, beyond acceptance, like a sea creature that should not exist.

Anders messaged in sick the first day. On the second he messaged to say he was more sick than he thought, and probably out for the week, upon which his boss called him, and when Anders did not answer, his boss messaged saying you better be dying, but he left Anders alone after that, other than, an hour later, sending a brief coda, you don't work, you don't get paid.

Anders had not yet seen anyone since he had changed, and he was not keen to see anyone, but he was out of milk and chicken breast and canned tuna, and there was only so much protein powder a man could reasonably be expected to consume, which meant he had to go out and face the world, or at least the clerk at the grocery store. He put on a cap and wedged it low.

His car, which had been his mother's car, was about half as old as he was, the workers who assembled it long retired, or made redundant, or replaced by robots, and it swayed a bit when it changed speed, and even more when it changed direction, like a dancer with a supple waist, or a drunk, but there was a pleasing responsiveness to its rebuilt engine, an eagerness to impress, and Anders's mother had been a fan of classical music, so his father had made certain the sound system was pure, with clear highs and an honest midrange, and what to Anders was, especially these days, a kind of understated, confident lack of boom in the bass.

In the parking lot of the grocery store he saw someone look at him, then look away, and it happened again in the dairy aisle. He did not know what they were thinking, if they were thinking anything, and he suspected it was only in his imagination that he saw flickers of hostility or distaste. He recognized the clerk who scanned his purchases but the clerk did not recognize him, and Anders had a moment of panic after he handed over his credit card, but the clerk did not glance at it, not at his name, not at his signature, and he did not acknowledge Anders's mumbled thanks and goodbye, did not budge or even blink, as though Anders had not spoken at all.

When Anders got back in his car it occurred to him that the three people he had seen were all white, and that he was perhaps being paranoid, inventing meaning out of details that might not matter, and at a traffic light he confronted his gaze in the rearview mirror, looked for the whiteness there, for it must be somewhere, maybe in his expression, but he could not see it, and the more he looked the less white he seemed, as though looking for his whiteness was the opposite of whiteness, was driving it further away, making him seem desperate, or uncertain, or like he did not belong, he who had been born here, damn it, and then he heard the loud continuous horn of the car to his rear, and he started to move past a signal that had some seconds ago turned green, and the woman behind him swerved to overtake, and rolled down her window, and cursed him, furious, cursed good and hard and sped off, and he did nothing, nothing, not shout back, not smile to disarm her, nothing, like he was mentally deficient, and she was pretty, really pretty, or had been before she shouted, and when he got home he wondered how he would have reacted, how he could have reacted, if there had only been some way for her to know he was white, or for him to know it, because suddenly, and there was no hiding from the full weight of this, he did not.

Anders took a hit of pot, held it tight in his lungs, but maybe this was a mistake, because by the time he had made himself lunch he was no longer hungry, instead he had a kind of strumming anxiety, which he knew from experience he had better smoke through, so as not to get stuck in it, and he smoked more, and stared at his phone, wandering around the internet, and in the end he had his lunch as his dinner.

Anders would have liked to speak to his mother, if there was one person in the world he could have talked to just then, it would have been her, but she was some years departed, from the water, they knew, the water that smelled wrong and tasted wrong, but then eventually got better, and so when the cancer came that ate her up from inside, like it ate up so many people, it was hard to prove there was a particular cause, hard to prove in court, anyway, and in her last months she could not talk, she could only rasp, and she wanted it to be over, so the ending was a blessing.

But before she had been sick she had listened, and she had boundless faith in her son, she had long conversations with him when he was late to speak, and she read to him in bed when he was late to read, and when he was in her classroom at the age of seven he loved it, so much so that the next year he refused to leave for the subsequent one, and stayed in her classroom for two weeks before he could be persuaded to agree, most reluctantly, to move on, and it was she who made him a reader, and fought for him to have extra time on his exams, and wanted him to attend college, though she had gone before he could go, and in the end life happened, and he had not gone, though he still, for her, but also for himself, hoped he might one day, or one night, as evening classes seemed more doable.

In high school people had always said that his best feature was his smile, an easy with myself and easy with you smile, a let's do this smile, generous, inviting, which had come to him from his mother, from her face to his, and now it was missing, the feeling that made it possible missing, and Anders did not know if it would ever return.

Two

When Oona answered the phone she had just finished meditating, and so she was in that fragile state of serenity that meditation can induce, the sense that one has briefly crested the wave of one's thoughts, and would like to remain here, like one is now, and already in desiring this, in desiring at all, one was slipping, losing one's buoyancy, dropping under the oncoming swell.

She heard the panic and anguish in Anders's voice with a flat rectangle of glass and metal pressed against the side of her head, cool then neutral in temperature, and she let him speak, and as he went on and on, she did try to reassure him, to be kind and supportive, but her heart was not really in it, a detachment had settled upon her, for as he was speaking, she was thinking mainly, and increasingly, of herself.

Oona had moved back to town to help her mother through the demise of Oona's twin brother, a demise long in coming, perhaps since that first pill at age fourteen, and she had moved back too on the off chance that her twin would want her with him when he ended, indeed that he could want in this way, that wants related to people could still surface in him strongly enough to overcome wants engineered by chemical dependencies, though to hope for this was to be outnumbered, to set the hope of one person against the industriousness of thousands, perhaps of millions, and her brother had died alone, as was always to be expected, not more than a few miles removed from kin.

So Oona did not berate herself for thinking of herself just then, as Anders spoke of his crisis. She was fond of Anders, but theirs was a high school attraction renewed recently, to her mind somewhat transaction-ally, as a way of passing the time, of getting through the time, and Oona did not reckon that she had much in reserve to expend on this new situation, she was cashed out, emotion-wise, and in fact deep into debt, focused for now on her own survival, her own being, and well within her rights to cut Anders off, to say she had to go, and avoid his calls for a bit, until the calls withered away, and that is what she planned to do when she said she had a class to teach, but then she surprised herself by adding, wearily, that she would come by to see him after work, this evening.

And she surprised herself even more by actually going.

—

The bicycle ride from her work took less than a quarter hour, progressing from the more prosperous to the poorer part of town, the sky not yet dark, but only the gas stations, the bars, the restaurants, and the convenience stores on her route still open, each of these numbering between a pair and a handful, no more than that. The share of empty storefronts grew as she went, and people seemingly ejected long ago by these derelict premises could be seen leaning against signposts on street corners and lying on cardboard in vacant lots.

Anders called his home his cabin, and it was small,

just a room, like a ground floor that should have led up to something else, but did not. Oona knocked hard on the flimsy door, banged really, then entered without waiting for a reply. It was rarely locked. She wanted to be the one seeing him, was less unsettled by that idea, the idea of finding him in the middle of doing whatever he was doing instead of waiting for him to present himself, this new version of himself, watching her for her reaction, but as it happened he was in the bathroom, so she found herself having to wait, uneasy, regardless.

The place was neat and orderly, everything put away where it belonged, not that Anders had many things except for books, of which he had an unusual quantity, or more than most young men, stacked against the walls on planks of wood and cinder blocks, the simplest possible bookshelves, reminding Oona of how bookish and methodical he had been as a teenager, such an unlikely, earnest reader.

When he emerged she was taken aback, not merely because he was darker, but because he was no longer recognizably himself, beyond being the same rough size and shape. Even the expression in his eyes was different, though maybe that was fear, his not hers, and it was only when he spoke and she heard his voice that she knew for certain, despite the fact that she had already been told, that it was indeed him.

"So you see?" he said.

"Damn," she replied.

He sat down on the sofa and after a moment's hesitation she went and sat next to him, and they spoke, and she could tell he was desperate for reassurance, but she was reluctant to provide it, resistant to being drawn into that role, yet again, not again, and resistant also to lying to him, because she did not know what good it would do, so she told him what she thought, flat-out, that he looked like another person, not just another person, but a different kind of person, utterly different, and that anyone who saw him would think the same, and it was hard, but there it was.

His eyes filled with tears but he did not cry, managed to keep them in his lashes, blinking and pursing his mouth, and then asked if she wanted a joint, even mustering a smile, to which she smiled back, a smile being a risk but slipping out of her anyway, and replied that, hell yes, she did.

He rolled and they smoked, as they often had, and they were quiet for a while, adrift, and then he nodded towards his bed and asked her to stay, and she thought about it, looking at him, still unnerved by his appearance, and even more by the woundedness and vulnerability of him, and when he got up and walked there, she did not follow, gave no sign, not until he started to undress, and then she did the same, warily, and they joined with a degree of caution, almost as though one was stalking the other, which of them stalking and which of them being stalked unclear, maybe both doing both, in a way, and so it was that they came to have that night's sex.

Anders worked at a gym and Oona taught yoga, and their bodies were youthful and fit, and if we, writing or reading this, were to find ourselves indulging in a kind of voyeuristic pleasure at their coupling, we could perhaps be forgiven, for they too were experiencing something not entirely dissimilar, pale-skinned Oona watching herself performing her grind with a dark-skinned stranger, Anders the stranger watching the same, and the performance was strong for them, visceral, touching them where, unexpectedly, or not so

unexpectedly, they discovered a jarring and discom-
forting satisfaction at being touched.

Afterwards, a curious sense of betrayal lingered, making sleep difficult for them both. Oona exited the bed
in the middle of the night, dressed, and walked out
without a word, unlocking her bicycle and pedaling
as quickly as she could. Anders's street was dark, and
even some of the main roads on her route had gaps in
their functioning streetlights like missing teeth. Had
she planned to stay this late, or leave this early, she
normally would have driven.

As Oona rode, she resisted the urge to look behind
her, or to look over at the pickup truck that, for a
while, coasted alongside, and when she got to her
house, she carried her bike up the porch steps, past the
signs for the neighborhood watch and the home secu-
rity company, and through the front door, where she
deposited it less temptingly in the entrance hall, and
then went upstairs, hearing the sound of her mother's
breathing, more an occasional gasp than a series of
snores, and arrived at last in her bedroom, which, like

19

the bedroom of her brother, had been left as she left it when she moved out, and even though upon her return Oona had removed the posters and stickers and school-age memorabilia, and replaced them with plants and photographs and work things, markers of her adult life, it still felt, in its bones, and in hers, like the room of a child.

When she woke, Oona saw she had a message from Anders and did not answer it. Instead she did her sun salutations, focused on her balance and what she called in her classes her ease, the naturalness and the smoothness of her movement. She detected a stiffness in herself, both physical and mental, a kind of tightness, or rigidity, which she set out to remedy through meditation, but thoughts of yesterday continued to intrude, so she attempted as best she could to bring mindfulness to the making of breakfast for herself and her mother, overnight oats with berries and nut butter, which her mother accepted with wonder and a shake of the head.

"It's so healthy it could kill a person," she said.

Oona raised an eyebrow. "That's the plan," she replied.

After they ate, Oona checked her mother's medications, one each for cholesterol, blood sugar, blood pressure, blood thinness, depression, and anxiety, to be taken in different quantities and combinations during the day. Her mother had once been the same height as Oona, but now was slightly shorter, and weighed twice as much, and looked significantly older than she was, though every so often when she napped her face could charge backwards through time and resemble, briefly, that of a baby.

"People are changing," her mother said.

"What people?" Oona asked.

"All over," she replied, and added with meaning, "our people."

It was the usual sort of thing, this time about white people suddenly not being white, and Oona saw another message from Anders alert itself to her on the screen of her phone, but she did not read it, and instead asked her mother how she knew this, and her mother said, from online, and Oona said she should not trust the stuff she found online, and initially said it honestly, out of habit, her voice solid with conviction, and it was only an instant later, when Oona thought about it, that she had to fabricate the sound of truth in her tone as she repeated herself.

Oona's mother had not been a fantasist when Oona and her brother were children, or rather, if she had, the fantasy she inhabited was a common one, the belief that life was fair and would turn out for the best and good people like them got what they deserved for the most part, exceptions being just that, exceptions, tragedies, but she had not worked after the twins were born, and when her husband had died, unexpectedly early, in the prime of health, he left her enough money to get by, but he took away that fantasy, leaving her alone to grapple with the slow loss of her son, in a world that did not care and was getting worse all the time, worse and worse, and more and more dangerous, a danger you could see all around you, all you had to do was to look at the crime and the potholes in the streets and the weird people who now came when you called for anything, for a plumber, an electrician, for help with your garden, for help with anything at all.

Oona was her mother's mother now, Oona sometimes felt, or maybe mother was not the right word for it, maybe daughter was fine, both words meaning more than she once thought they did, each having two sides to itself, a side of carrying and a side of being carried, each word in the end the same as the other, like a coin, differing only in the order of what face came up first on a toss.

Oona heard her mother out, knowing that to argue was to prolong, to engage was to lose, and when her mother could see she would not get the satisfaction of a disagreement, she glanced in the direction of the room with the big television, and Oona put on her backpack, took hold of her bike, and headed for the door.

"You're so beautiful," her mother said as she was leaving. "You should get a gun."

Three

That week Anders felt vaguely menaced as he went around town, which he did as little as he could manage, and though this carried its own risks he wore a hoodie, his face invisible from the sides, and if it had been colder on those glorious, early autumn days, he would have worn gloves, but that would have looked ridiculous given the temperature, so he kept his hands in his pockets and a backpack slung over one shoulder to carry whatever he had come out to get, rolling paper or bread or a replacement charging cable for his phone, meaning his hands could mostly stay hidden, slipping out only to open a door or slide across a payment, a flash of brown skin like a fish darting up to the surface and down again, aware of the hazards of being seen.

People who knew him no longer knew him. He passed them in his car or on the sidewalk, where sometimes they gave him extra room, and where sometimes, unthinkingly, he did the same. No one hit him or knifed him or shot him, no one grabbed him, no one even shouted at him, not after the woman in the car, at least not yet, and Anders was not sure where his sense of threat was coming from, but it was there, it was strong, and once it was obvious to him that he was a stranger to those he could call by name, he did not try to look in their faces, to let his gaze linger in ways that could be misconstrued.

Almost as disturbing as seeing someone he recognized was the feeling of being recognized by someone he did not, someone dark, waiting at a bus stop or wielding a mop or sitting in a group at the back of a pickup truck, sitting in a group that was, he could not help it, that was like a group of animals, not like humans, being transported from one task, one site, to the next, and actually this was more disturbing, the moment when one dark man would look at him, look at Anders as though he saw him, for an instant, their eyes meeting, not in friendliness or hostility, but just as people's eyes meet, as people, and when this happened Anders would look quickly away.

Anders put off telling his father, why he was not sure, maybe because his father had always seemed a little disappointed in him, and this would add to his disappointment, or maybe because his father had enough on his plate, and Anders did not want to in-crease his burden, or maybe because until his father was told, it would not have really happened, Anders would still be Anders, there in the house where he grew up, and the telling would undo that, and make everything different, irrevocably different, but what-ever the reason, he waited, he waited and then he told.

He did it over the phone, which was a cowardly thing to do, but he had no idea how to drop by and just say it, why his father would even believe him, and that was how he had told Oona, over the phone, and so that was how he did it again, and his father hung up the first time, and the second time asked him if he was high, if he thought this was a joke, and when Anders said no to both, he asked, with steel in his voice, a steel familiar to Anders, if his son was trying to call him a racist, to which Anders replied he most definitely was not, and so his father said, show me, smart guy, come here and show me if you can.

Anders's father had beaten him properly only once, he had hit him more than a few times, but a solid beating, that was only once, for his mother had long forbidden it, and the time he had beaten Anders it was because Anders had been negligent with a loaded rifle, discharging it by mistake, Anders negligent after repeatedly being warned, and back then Anders was two heads shorter than his father, and his father, Anders thought, had been right to beat him, but it had been a beating Anders would never forget, not the beating nor the lesson, and that was the point, a gun was a marker on the journey of death, and was to be respected as such, like a coffin or a grave or a meal in winter, not to be foolish with, and as he drove to his father now, though Anders was the taller, heavier man, for some reason that beating found its way right into the front of Anders's mind.

Anders's father was a construction foreman, gaunt and ill to his core, ill in his guts, but he did not trust doctors and refused to see them, and his pale eyes burned like he had a fever, or like he was praying for

28

a murder, they had been that way since Anders's mother had died, or since she had gotten sick and it had become clear she would not get better, or maybe since before that, Anders was not sure, but for all his gauntness his back was erect and his forearms were like corded ropes, and he could walk carrying an improbable load and barely sway, with the kind of strength that just got things done, a fearsome strength, if Anders was honest, and his father was waiting for him on the stoop of his house, and he was looking at his son, the son who had reminded him of his wife, the boy's mother, not that the boy was soft, but he was gentler than was good for him, and he was lost in dreams too easily, and he had her fine stamp on him, a boy in his mother's mold, and as he saw his boy now, as he watched Anders approach, that was all gone, she was gone, and this boy, who made easy things hard, who had not yet found his way, this boy, Anders's father could see, was going to suffer, and his mother had vanished, she was nowhere to be glimpsed in him, and he stood there, Anders's father, a cigarette in his mouth, one hand holding on to the fabric of his son's sleeve, the other rigid at his side, and he wept, he wept like a shudder, like an endless cough, without a sound, staring at the man who had been Anders, until his son took him inside, and they both at last sat down.

———

On her day off, Oona went to the city to see a friend, the city where she had gone to college and begun an interrupted, or abandoned, life, Oona was not sure which, she had once thought the former, but she was a realist, and she knew every month you spent away from the city made it harder ever to return, she knew that, the city just worked that way, it was the price you had to be prepared to pay, and she was prepared, mostly, and she was paying it, but she missed the city, missed it fiercely, especially then, as she drove the three-hour drive that day and let herself feel it calling.

Crossing the bridge and the mighty water and seeing the tall buildings, it was as though she was entering another world, and becoming another Oona, and it should not have been possible that she could just pull over and step out of her car onto these streets she knew so well, but it was, and she walked in her old neighborhood park, and grabbed a bottle of wine from her old liquor store, and saw the lights start to glow against the evening, and then she was in her friend's tiny apartment and the wine was open and the city was there outside the windows and they could have pretended, if they cared to, that no time had passed for them at all.

But they spoke, and Oona did not want to speak of her brother, but her friend asked, and so she did, and the mood changed, and it was now again, and not then. They had to eat, which took them out, and as they ate, they drank, and their spirits grew less heavy, and they went to a bar Oona had never been to before, and they drank further, and guys hit on them, and there was dancing, and there was a body close to hers, and being touched through the fabric of her dress, and a proposition, and a shared rhythm, and considering whether to go home with him, more than considering, the up-close beginnings of something, desire, but there was tiredness too, a tiredness, and an excuse made, about an early start to the next day, and an unsettled sleep on her friend's sleeping bag, on a sliver of bare floor, and an alarm at dawn, she who never needed an alarm, and then she was on the highway, a large coffee having replaced her usual morning ritual, under a bloody sky, her mind full and aching, the music low, headed back to make it in time for her noon class, to teach, to dig into herself to be able, and teach.

That week Anders messaged Oona and she only inter-mittently replied, from his end enough for him to try again a day or two later, from hers enough not to seem completely cold, the fact that she was messaging him to any extent being against her better judgment, and she was careful not to message so readily as to imply she was more comfortable with his situation than she was, which was to say not very comfortable at all.

Reports began to emerge from around the country of people changing, reports at first utterly disreputable, and easily disregarded, and roundly mocked, rightly so, but later picked up by reliable voices, as a question to be confirmed, being confirmed, apparently happening.

When Oona's mother called her downstairs one night to say that it was on the television, that they were interviewing someone who had stopped being white, right now, on the news, and then said, as Oona stood beside her, you see, you see, there's proof, Oona watched, and after a while stepped out and phoned Anders.

Behind Oona's house the moon was visible, a little less than full, a pregnant belly moon, that was what her father used to call it, and stars were scattered across the sky, and Jupiter was there, bright, and Saturn, not quite so much, and she followed their arc, looking for Mars, but there were trees in the way, and Mars was nowhere to be seen, and not seeing Mars made her think of how frigid space was, how inhuman, a lifeless void, dead, like her father, and like her brother who had followed him, who had never gotten over him, and this train of thought unmoored her, making the Earth less reliable an anchor, her connection to the grass under her bare feet less firm, and she felt the pull of their absence, her brother, her father, pulling at her, the nothingness that had taken them, that takes us all, how can it take us all, obliterating us, and then a ringing, a ringing that stopped, and Anders answered her.

He had been watching the news too.

"I guess you're not alone," she said.

"I guess not," he replied, quietly.

"How does that feel?" she asked.

He waited a long time. "Not worse," he said. And the way he said it, it sounded to her like an invitation.

Four

To his boss, Anders explained his situation, which was not unique, nor contagious, as far as anyone knew, and returned to the gym after a week off, and his boss was waiting for him at the entrance, bigger than Anders remembered him, though obviously the same size, and his boss looked him over and said, "I would have killed myself."

Anders shrugged, unsure how to reply, and his boss added, "If it was me."

Though it smelled of sweat, the gym was empty, it being early, the steel racks and wood-floored platforms and benches with duct-taped tears in their upholstery all unoccupied, and the two of them worked out separately, Anders's boss clanging through monster sets on the squat, thick, his elbows like knees, his knees like heads, his face red with rage, as it was whenever he lifted heavy, reminding Anders of the time a few months ago when his boss almost attacked someone who talked to him at a meet, talked to him at the wrong moment, when he was in his zone, the berserker zone he inhabited just before an attempt, for even in middle age his boss was still a serious competitor, in the masters category, and how his boss had to be restrained, with great difficulty, by four large men, men far larger than Anders, and Anders was there, close by, not to compete but just to support, and the whole incident had left him uneasy, there being something primal about it, unsettling, and he was reminded of it just then, as in between sets his boss stopped, stopped and watched Anders deadlift, Anders reaching his work weight, a weight no more or less than Anders had done before, which was reassuring to Anders, in a way, it was something that had not changed, but he wondered if his boss felt differently, given how intensely he was watching, if he expected the weight would be different, because Anders was different, or if all this was just in Anders's mind, and regardless he was relieved when the first client entered the space, and there were three of them there, not two.

The gym filled as the day progressed, and Anders did not want to, but he started to notice stares, quick, evasive stares, as word spread, that he, this dark guy, was Anders, had been Anders, and Anders tried to ignore it, for he was popular at the gym, the person you went to when you had a pain in your knee or when you could not reach readily overhead, when you had pushed too hard, when a lifetime of aches had gotten the better of you, which was often, because this was a black iron gym, a rough gym, where men, and it was usually only men, tested themselves with barbells against gravity, not some shiny place with chrome-plated machines, and the clients skewed older here, and they pushed not like they were exercising but like they were desperate, and so they valued Anders, whom the old-timers called doc, short for doctor, because in his years here he had become a bit of an expert in putting bodies back together, and read all he could find to read, was a kind of dedicated, erudite tinkerer, and so people liked him, they liked him a lot, in this gym, or they had, for it did not quite feel that way now, it did not feel entirely comfortable, it felt, if Anders was honest, unless he was being paranoid, maybe he was being paranoid, sort of on edge.

Anders told himself the stares were natural, anyone would have done the same, he would have done the same, it was not a regular situation, after all, and to reassure people, and to reassure himself too, he tried to engage in his normal banter, to be, as it were, like himself, to act undeniably like himself, but this was more difficult than he had imagined, impossible really, for what was more unlike oneself, more awkward, than trying to be oneself, and it was throwing him off, this artificiality, but he had no idea what to replace it with, and so he began instead to mirror the others around him, to echo the way they spoke and walked and moved and the way they held their mouths, like they were performing something, and he was trying to perform it too, and what it was he did not know, but whatever it was it was not enough, or his performance of it was off, because his sense of being observed, of being on the outside, looked at by those who were in, of messing things up for himself, deeply frustrating, did not go away all day.

———

Oona spent that day at her studio, her clients quite different from those of Anders, mostly women, and while not wealthy, wealthier by local standards, and more educated, staving off aging through attempts to remain supple, and relatively slender, in surroundings where human smells were banished, and those inspired by plants were introduced in their place, connoting, perhaps, Oona thought, the natural cycle of life or, conversely, come to think of it, immortality, like a redwood forest, whose trees could live almost forever.

Oona was the most junior of the primary instructors at the studio, and she was in demand because she was diligent and talented, and because she looked the part, her body the sort of body her clients ascribed legitimacy to, and if she was not overly friendly, then at least she was not unfriendly, which was fair enough, given the recent tragedy in her family, the story of which had been widely discussed among the studio regulars.

Unlike Anders, Oona did not know if she wanted

what she was doing to remain her career. Teaching
yoga had begun as what she did on the side, but on the
side of what was never clear, not finding in the city a
supposedly real job that stuck, or a vocation that felt
like her unambiguous calling, after dabbling in acting
and writing and even in a start-up, but without making
much headway in any of these, and for a time she had
considered trying to monetize herself through social
media, posting images of her day and her practices and
her life, but while she was followed, she was not followed sufficiently, and she had wondered if it was that
she was not attractive enough, or not skilled enough
in photography, or if she seemed fake, if her fakeness
was less hidden than that of others, and while thousands of strangers seemed content to gaze upon her, it
was not hundreds of thousands, or millions, or even
the tens of thousands that would mark real progress,
and seemed it never would be, and the constant curat-
ing of herself deprived her of some of the satisfaction
she genuinely did find in yoga, and when her brother
died she had stopped posting, and felt no wish to post
more now, though she did not delete her account, just
left it there, a door back to the potentially addictive

quest for celebrity, like a cigarette in the home of someone who has quit, and is successfully managing the quitting, but feels warmly about the part of themselves that felt warmly about being a smoker.

When her work was done that night, Oona biked home and ate dinner with her mother, and her mother barely ate anything, which meant she had probably already eaten, though her mother denied this, denied it with a persecuted tone that suggested it was true, and her mother complained of pain, the one complaint Oona and she had both agreed she would not treat with strong medication, because of what it had done to Oona's brother, but they each had a glass of wine, and afterwards Oona drew her mother a bath, with candles and spoonfuls of effervescent powder, and helped her mother step over the edge, to make sure she did not fall again, entry to the bathtub being trickier than to the shower stall, and then left the room while her mother waited to remove her short robe, unlike when Oona was a child and her mother had stripped and bathed before her without a second thought, a new modesty born of horror, and when she was finished, Oona sat by her mother's bed and massaged her soft, rough feet with lotion, and then slipped outside, optimistic that her mother would fall asleep, which she had been unable to do the night before, not properly, only managing a couple of disturbed hours, but when Oona checked a few minutes later it had happened, the sound was unmistakable, the briefest of solitary gasps, a victory, and Oona should have been ready for bed herself, but she was not ready, she was off center, jangled, and so she did not go to bed, she went downstairs and drove unannounced to see Anders.

Oona did not feel that she wanted to be touched, that she wanted physical release, she wanted something else, company maybe, yes, his company, Anders's company, to sit with him, understood, and simply be.

What had happened to Anders almost dissuaded her halfway, stopped at a red light, but she did not turn back, and then she arrived, and his door was, as always, unlocked, and with a couple of warning bangs she was inside, and the dark man was there, the dark man who had been Anders, and she had seen him once before, this dark man, even had sex with him once before, bizarre now to think, but it was as if she was seeing him for the first time, an unknown person, and she had to will herself to see Anders in him, to see that this was Anders, the Anders she was familiar with, had spent many nights with, over these past months, this was that Anders, Anders on his clunky old computer, tapping with it perched on his lap, looking up at her, and smiling a smile she did not recognize, not on him, not yet, but a smile that did not intensify the force she felt eroding her, a smile that stood by itself and did not demand.

They listened to music and smoked a joint, Anders on the sofa, Oona on the floor, the distance and difference in elevation precluding unconscious touching, so they touched only when passing, fingers grazing fingers, and they spoke a little but not too much, Anders surprised and pleased to have her there, but worried by her presence too, worried by the ease with which it could be lost, and by what it meant to be worried about such a thing, and Oona did not know she had been waiting, but it seemed she had, for she began to speak, and once she began, for a long time she did not stop.

Oona told a tale of tadpoles, of missions to the pond to collect them, the pond near what they called the waterfall, a concrete cliff about as high as an adult, over which the creek gushed when it had rained, and trickled when it had not, and in the pond were tadpoles, which her brother loved to catch with a net meant for aquarium fish, but first there was the dotted jelly of the eggs, and then the smallest wriggling forms, and then on the next trip proper-sized tadpoles, but still they would wait, wait until their forelegs had begun to grow, until the first nubs, the stumps, came, and that was when her brother liked to collect them, always a pair, called him and her, though they did not know if they were, and could not tell one from the other, collected then because they were more interesting at that stage, and could be watched in a tank of pond water at home, their forelegs growing, their tails shrinking, with a plan to return them before their tails had vanished, before the tadpoles were frogs and would drown, a well-considered plan that never worked, not in all the times they tried it, not once, which sounds horrible now, but was just sad then, we were sad for them, as if it was not our fault they died, and with that

Oona was finished, and when she finished she got up and touched her cheek, wondering if she would find it wet, but there were no tears there, and her voice was steady, so she concluded she had not cried, and she left Anders with a small wave goodbye.

Five

Anders's boss had said he would have killed himself, and the following week a man in town did just that, his story followed by Anders in the local press, or rather online in the regional section of a large publication, the local paper having shut down long ago, this man shooting himself in front of his own house, a shooting heard but not seen by a neighbor, and called in, and assumed to be an act of home defense, the dark body lying there an intruder, shot with his own gun after a struggle, but the homeowner was not present, and was nowhere to be found, and then the wedding ring and the wallet and the phone on the dead man were all tallied up, and the messages that had been sent, and the experts weighed in, and the sum of it all was clear, in other words that a white man had indeed shot a dark man, but also that the dark man and the white man were the same.

The mood in town was changing, more rapidly than its complexion, for Anders could not as yet perceive any real shift in the number of dark people on the streets, or if he could, he could not be sure of it, those who had changed still being, by all accounts, few and far between, but the mood, yes, the mood was changing, and the shelves of the stores were more bare, and at night the roads were more abandoned, and even the days were shorter and cooler than they had been only recently, the leaves no longer as confident in their green, and while these seasonal shifts were perhaps only the course of things, the course of things felt to Anders more fraught.

At work, Anders had become quieter than he used to be, less sure of how any action of his would be perceived, and it was like he had been recast as a supporting character on the set of the television show where his life was being enacted, but even so he had not yet lost all hope that a return to his old role was possible, to his old centrality, or if not centrality, then at least to a role better than this peripheral one, and so he was almost excited to hear that a long-standing client of the gym had changed, in fact was excited, was awaiting his arrival with some eagerness, now Anders would not be the only one, excited until the man came at the time he was expected, a dark man recognizable only by his jacket, and he stood there, this man, looking around, looking at those looking at him, and left without a word, as though he might never, no, would never, return.

Oona's mother was active online, and listened to the radio, and watched the news, and she had come to believe that she was on the inside, among the elect, those who understood the plot, the plot her daughter said was ridiculous, a plot that had been building for years, for decades, maybe for centuries, the plot against their kind, yes their kind, no matter what her daughter said, for they had a kind, the only people who could not call themselves a people in this country, and there were not so many of them left, and now it had arrived, and was upon them, and she was afraid, for what could she do, but there were those among them who would stand up, stand up and protect her, and she had to believe in them, and be ready, be ready as best she could, to preserve herself, and especially her daughter, her daughter who was the future, was the future of everything, for without her daughter, without all their daughters, they would be lost, a field with no shoots, no saplings, no life, a desert, covered in sand, with lizards from far away scampering about, and strange cactus growing where once there were hearty crops, and she had not wished to live in such times, it frightened her, she was terrified, but she was fated to, as her ancestors had been fated to live in eras of war and plague and calamity, and she had to be worthy of her roots, and pull herself together, pull through, for her daughter, for herself, for her people, and do what must be done.

Provisions were needed, and she had already hesitated too long, and bought too little, bought too little because she had too little money, what her husband had left was only just enough, and some years it seemed it would run out prematurely, and some years it seemed it would last, but with no margin for error, and in all years she was careful with it, mending her own clothes, moderating the heating, finding good deals, avoiding the frivolous, except rarely, very rarely, when she could not help it, like with her television, which was larger than she absolutely needed, but was so important that she had allowed herself the indulgence, and even then purchased it secondhand, from a shop that stood by it, and guaranteed it with a warranty, and now she needed provisions, enough to last a long time, and they would cost money, and throw off her budget, throw it off completely, and so she had hesitated, but she knew she could hesitate no more.

Oona tried to dissuade her, to say a little extra was sensible, but this much was not, this much was too much, and their arguments grew heated, and when she drove with her mother to the big stores outside town where purchases could be made in bulk, Oona did not let her mother listen to the radio stations she wanted to listen to, and attempted to bring a dose of reality to the proceedings, and wondered about her mother's sanity, and even about her own, for her mother was convinced, and would not be dissuaded, and was buttressed in her conviction by the lines of shoppers who evidently thought as her mother did, items running out, not just food but batteries and bandages and medicines, and much else besides, and the more her mother bought, the more Oona bought with her mother, the more it alarmed Oona, the more it made her doubt, and feel uncertain, feel less confident that her mother was wrong, less able to say, for sure, that it was not on its way, crazy, crazy, but perhaps perceptible on the breeze nonetheless, perhaps coming, though it could not possibly be coming, a great, a terrible, storm.

Oona and Anders went for a walk, and Oona told him about her mother's obsession with being prepared, and their recent shopping expeditions, and about all the hoarding she had seen, the way people were hoarding, and Anders said maybe he ought to stockpile a bit too, maybe there would be disruptions, but he hoped things would settle down, did she think things would settle down, and she said she did, and then she said she did not know anymore, and he said he did not know anymore either, he had thought it would all blow over, eventually, but to be honest, he did not know.

They were walking alongside a stream, a stream that ran by their old high school, the stream subdued now, in autumn, and they were winding through the rough between a parking lot and the water, opposite to the school, broken bottles and bits of rubbish scattered on the gravel path, and Anders liked this area, not obviously appealing in itself, because it reminded him of joints and drunken rambles with buddies he wished he had not drifted away from, and Oona liked it because she used to walk here with her brother, together cutting class, and just then the sun was out, and the tall wetland weeds, the cattails, were swaying in the wind, a wind with the hint of a nip, but they were dressed appropriately, Anders and Oona, they were ready for it, and it was not so bad at all.

Oona felt the coolness on her face, awakening her skin, and they walked, and then Anders said that he was not sure he was the same person, he had begun by feeling that under the surface it was still him, who else could it be, but it was not that simple, and the way people act around you, it changes what you are, who you are, and Oona said she understood, that it was like learning a foreign language, and when you tried to speak a foreign language, you lost your sense of humor, no matter how much you tried, you could not be funny the way you used to be, and Anders said he did not know a foreign language, it had been hard enough for him to read and write in their language, and he laughed and she laughed with him, and he said, but I get what you mean, yes that is exactly it.

A heavy truck rumbled over a pothole, somewhere in the distance, and as the echoes of the dull booms faded, Anders said that there was a dark-skinned cleaning guy at the gym, he worked nights, and Anders had always been nice to him, but the cleaning guy had started to look at him in a new way after Anders changed, and Anders had not liked it, but it got him thinking, and he had realized that the cleaning guy was the only guy at the gym who never exercised there, and he was such a small guy, and was he hired because of that, because he was small, in a place where it was important to be big, and did he have a family, back where he came from, or was he alone, and why had Anders never asked him these things, and why did the new way he looked at Anders bother Anders, the way he looked at Anders like Anders could talk to him,

but Anders had not yet talked to him, not beyond the
usual hey there, have a good one, and Anders had
decided he would talk to him, finally after all these
years, he would stop being nice to him, which was not
really being nice to him, it was just treating the cleaning guy like a puppy, a dog, that you give a couple pats
to, and call out good boy, and instead Anders would
talk to him, and see what he had to say, not because
Anders was better than before, but because the way
Anders saw stuff was not the same, because the cleaning guy could probably tell Anders a few things, and
Anders could probably stand to learn.

The mosquitoes were gone, and the dragonflies
too, the air above the stream sieved of its swarms of
insects, sieved by fall, and high overhead birds were
winging their way to warmer climes, and it was the
kind of day when the planet could be felt making its
journey, tilted and spinning as it went, never still, un-
stoppable, calling afternoons forth from mornings.

Oona glanced at Anders and reflected in silence
that sometimes he looked normal to her, and sometimes strange, her perception flipping, kind of like
when you stared at a blank television screen, a screen

showing static, and after a while you started to see images, weird images like snakes or waves or a mountain, or no, not quite like that, for it was not his face but more her sense of it that reversed, from one minute to the next, more like a carton of milk that you sniffed and found had gone bad, but then tasted fine, if you took a sip a moment later.

It was a day off, and they had casually aligned their schedules to have this day off coincide, eager to meet in sunlight, elsewhere than at Anders's place, without the pressures and complications of a bed nearby. It was not a day off at school, but some schoolboys were standing on the opposite bank, one of them smoking, another skipping stones, and the boys did not stare at Anders and Oona as they approached, but they did look, and the boys were all a similar color, more or less, and Anders was dark and Oona was light, and Anders and Oona became intensely aware of their difference in that instant, and the boy who was skipping did not pause his skipping, and the sharp flat stones he threw were not necessarily round, and some went farther than others, and one could have crossed over to Anders and Oona, and thudded into the path as they walked, but no stone hit them, or came particularly close, and Oona did not know if this was by chance or design, and Anders gazed straight ahead, not locking eyes with the boys, not challenging the throwing, which did not stop, as it might have, given the risk of error or misunderstanding.

PART
TWO

There were flare-ups of violence in town, a brawl here, a shooting there, and the mayor repeatedly called for calm, but militants had begun to appear on the streets, pale-skinned militants, some dressed almost like soldiers in combat uniform, or halfway like soldiers, with military-style trousers and civilian jackets, and others dressed like hunters, in woodland colors, or in jeans and ammunition vests, but all the militants, whatever their attire, visibly armed, and as for the police, the police made no real effort to stop them.

The militants did not confront Oona when, on occasion, she ran into them. They did not hassle her, no more than a group of men might normally hassle a woman out on her own, even less, possibly because she was white, or because they figured she supported them, for she wore no sign or badge of her disapproval and kept her mouth shut, but she had lingered too late at her share of drunken parties in high school and college, and she knew the feeling the militants gave her, the feeling that they were together and she was alone, and that her situation could change in an instant, and she did not bike anymore, she drove, and they frightened her.

But her mother seemed positively jolly, on a high, as though she had just heavily upped her mood medications, and her body had not yet had time to downregulate its own systems in response, and Oona had not seen her like this since Oona's brother had died, maybe not since Oona's father had died, she looked as though all was well with the world, and the planet was headed in the right direction, and wrongs would be righted, and the future was bright, with grounds for optimism again, grounds for optimism after forever.

Oona remembered doing molly with her brother a few months post their father's funeral, back when they were in high school, and they had done molly before, and her brother had not been so bad then, he was just one of those kids who liked to dabble in substances, somewhat regularly, and he had not yet found the substances that would hook him, and Oona had thought it might be too soon after their father to do the molly, and for her it had been, she had become miserable, but her brother had not, he had looked joyous, joyous but brittle, his joy both powerful and forced, like Oona's mother's was now, and it was possible that her brother's brittleness that day had to do with his twin sister's low, with having to manage her, but Oona thought not, she thought her brother had been brittle because he could not fully fool himself, because he was going to break, had already broken, like her mother had broken, and joy like that when you had broken, that kind of sudden, crazy joy, unearned, that was just a mask.

So Oona worried for her mother, who was disconcertingly unworried now, or anyway less worried now, which in her mother was strange indeed, and Oona worried for herself, for their town, and for Anders, more than she might have expected for Anders, and she redoubled her commitment to her meditation practice, with decidedly mixed results, the churn in her mind often being too strong.

———

Anders went to see his father on a day with some chill in it, using the back roads, proceeding hesitantly, pausing and observing at intersections, like a herbivore, out of an instinct for self-preservation, ascertaining what was ahead before he moved, and he had gloves on his hands and a hoodie over his head and sunglasses over his eyes, ineffectual concealment, but perhaps enough, from a distance, and it was not that he had been threatened, for he had not been, not yet, but just that he felt threatened, and so he was taking no chances, or none that he could avoid.

His father was slow to answer when Anders knocked on his door, and Anders was struck by how much his father had deteriorated in the weeks since Anders had seen him last, and the son knew for certain that the father was leaving now, knew that this mighty, skinny man was on his way out, nearly gone, and Anders was glad for his sunglasses, so that his father would not have to see the knowledge enter Anders's eyes, and his father was bent over, just a bit, he who had always stood so straight, bent as though his illness had punched him in the stomach that morning and he did not want to show that the blow continued to hurt, but when something so straight and so important is bent, even just a bit, it is remarkable to behold, and Anders beheld it, and they shook hands, their grips firm, firmer than usual, to compensate for the infirmity, and Anders's father did not like to look at Anders, at what his son had become, and he did not like that he did not like it, and so he forced himself to look at his son, to hold on to his son's hand even longer, the brown skin against his pale skin, and he clapped Anders on the shoulder and squeezed him there, for Anders's father an expressive gesture, and he inclined his head in welcome and took his darkened son back home.

Inside the house, the furnishings were dated, and did not match Anders's father, what he would have bought for himself, for they had been bought by Anders's mother, and reminded Anders of her, the little frills on the sofa covers, the lace coasters on the side tables, and in the living room the photos were of all of them, of Anders's parents as young people, of

Anders as a baby and as a boy, of the family together, none more recent than about a decade ago, photos already aged by the passage of time.

Anders's father listened as his son told him of his unease, and he watched his son drink a beer while he let his own sit, barely sipped, his beer there out of habit and propriety, because Anders's father could no longer manage the drinking of it, and he fetched the metal flask with his cash in it and gave money to his son, over his son's objections, and he went through his cupboards and helped his son load some essential supplies in his car, or handed them to his son, anyway, the boy would have to do the work, standing was hard enough, and he ignored his pain, for it was part of him now, constant, not remotely bearable, but also not avoidable, and so put up with, like a nasty sibling, and he retrieved a rifle and a box of shells, and he outlasted his boy's reluctance, saying take it and waiting, and he witnessed his boy do what his boy needed to do, which was to stop pretending, and to start to accept the situation, and to receive what his father was holding, what was obviously needed, and his boy grew serious as he held the weight of the rifle and the shells, which was good, seriousness was what the situation required.

Once returned to his own home, Anders wondered whether the rifle actually made him safer, for he felt he was all alone, and it was better to be non-confrontational than to stand up to trouble, and he imagined that somehow people were more likely to come for him if they found out he was armed, even though they would not find out, even though so many folks were armed, he just had this sense that it was essential not to be seen as a threat, for to be seen as a threat, as dark as he was, was to risk one day being obliterated.

Anders knew he would soon lose his father, and that impending loss seemed more concrete now, more real, not like air but like a door or a wall, something you could bang against, bang into, and of course children know they will lose their parents, they know it from early on, but most are able to believe that that particular present will not come, that it is years away, and between every year there are months, and between every month there are days, and between every day there are hours, and between every hour there are seconds, and so on, the instants that are left stretching out into infinity, and Anders had lost a parent already, and had experienced the reality that the time we have is not limitless, but prior to today he had not yet had that moment with his father, that moment of realization that the end was close, and now that he had had it, he was in a pensive mood, and Oona's arrival in his home, when she came, was more than a relief, it was a possibility.

Oona too felt something different, not just in Anders, for she saw there was something different in him, but in herself, in the way she was drawn to him, not as a silencing of what she did not want to hear, not only that, not anymore, but as an opportunity to speak, as a beginning rather than the managing of an end, and maybe the fact that Anders no longer looked like Anders allowed her to see her relationship with him in another way, or maybe the fact that Anders remained Anders regardless of what he looked like allowed her to see the Anders in him more clearly, but whatever it was, she was glad to be there with him, glad and human, her need not mechanical, not a mechanism, but organic, and so more complicated, and also more fertile.

Oona sat next to him and they talked and they smoked and they kissed, and the kiss was a proper kiss, a hello kiss, and when they had sex it was as though it was the first time they were having sex, for the first time they had actually had sex Oona was not looking, she was looking only within, and the first time they had sex after Anders changed, it had not been Anders and Oona having sex, it had been other than that, others, but this time Anders saw Oona, and Oona saw Anders, and the sex was slow, unhurried, a languid, naked sex, a once or twice grinning sex, with its urgencies fully visible, its frowns, its expressions of pain, its instinctive anguishes unhidden, and if they were performing, their performance was an attempt at naturalness, and in their attempt they came close, closer than they had come before.

Seven

At work Anders was no longer the only one who had changed, there were others, beyond that first other who had come once and then disappeared, and a gym that had been almost a whites-only gym, almost, now had not one dark man present, nor two, those two being Anders and, in the evenings, the cleaning guy, but often three, or even four, and Anders had thought this would make things better, but it seemed the opposite was happening, and the gym was increasingly tense, and men who had known each other for years now acted like they did not know each other, or worse, disliked each other, bore a grudge, and in the violence of a heavy lift, within that violence, the battle of a man straining alone with hundreds of pounds on his back, or at his feet, or above his chest, there was greater violence, and less caution, and self-induced injuries from excessive loads that compromised form were becoming noticeably more common.

The cleaning guy held down two jobs, and he arrived a couple of hours before closing time, and he did the entrance first, and then the offices in the rear, and he began on the main area of the gym half an hour before it shut, when it was not too crowded, but the people who remained were usually die-hards, and irritable at the ends of their series of sets, and Anders observed that the cleaning guy always gave the stations still in use a wide berth, mopping around them, leaving dry islands, and keeping low, which was not hard for him, since he was a small fellow, and Anders found himself thinking of a bird perched next to lions, like a vulture, or not a vulture, maybe a crow, belonging to another element, the air, but feeding at the same place as the predators of the land, except that this bird could not fly, and it was unsafe in case of trouble, and counted precariously on being ignored.

The back of the gym, the changing rooms and

lockers and showers, stayed open a little longer, and one night as Anders was ready to leave, two men got into an argument, and they took it outside, and they were older guys, but big, bulky and strong and surprisingly quick despite their bellies, and they started to shove each other in the parking lot, and a few people gathered round, but those who gathered did not say anything, that was what struck Anders, they did not tell the two to stop, nor cheer them on, they were silent, they just watched, and soon the two men were punching, and it was ferocious, and out of the grunts and the shuffles came the sound of a fist hitting the side of a face, the solid crack of it, the thud, softly liquid and bone breaking at the same time, such a visceral, disturbing sound that it made Anders turn away, and he walked off, walked off without seeing what happened next, whether the dark one had the better of it or the pale one, Anders did not want to see, and though he did not see, the sound lingered, and it kept coming to him even as he lay in his bed that night, causing a wince, or a grimace, a physical response, Anders twitching there by himself, in echo.

The following night Oona joined Anders in his bed, and stayed there until morning, and in the morning when she woke he was sleeping, and there was something ridiculous about his posture, a mismatch between his sprawled-out body and his tightly closed face, his face serious in a dream, like he was attending a business meeting, but his scattered limbs as free as those of a child, or of a teenager, one calf over her shin, the back of one hand against her belly, his bare knuckles grazing her bare navel where her t-shirt had ridden up, making her conscious of her breath, and she followed her breathing, through her nostrils, down, touching him there, her swelling into him, cushioning him, and then up again, and when eventually he opened his eyes he glimpsed an expression in hers he had not seen before, an almost baffled tenderness, and it caused him to cock his head and smile and wait and then give her a kiss.

"How scared are you of dying?" she asked him.

"Good morning to you too," he replied.

She laughed and came closer to him, wrapping a

leg around his, and she said she thought of dying a lot, not her dying, necessarily, just people dying, though her dying also, and he nodded, and he said when his mother was dying he had been certain she would not die, certain until he was not certain, and when he finally knew she was dying, was not sick but dying, he saw how much she wanted to live, until the pain took that from her, and she wanted to go, or did not want to go, but needed to go, needed to go even more than she wanted to stay, and he had not been ready for that, for his mother to need to leave, and it was a terrible thing to see.

She said her father had gone without warning, it had been preposterous, no other word for it, here he was, and then he was gone, and it had made her think there was a trapdoor under each of us, a trapdoor that could open at any second, like we were walking on a bridge of ropes and planks, swaying high above a canyon, and some of the planks were rotten, and you could take a normal step but find that you had stepped into nothingness, without even hearing the snap, and that realization should have caused you to be more careful, to step lightly, but it had not done that to her brother, he had stomped on the planks, harder and harder, as though he was fine with breaking them, as though part of him wanted to go, maybe like Anders's mother had wanted to go, but without the pain, or no, not without the pain, but without that kind of pain, without cancer, just with heartbreak, since the universe had let him down, and it had shown him it was not the kind of universe he could love, it was a universe that betrayed us, all of us, and so he had decided to leave, or not decided, it was not a decision, it was a direction, a shift in his direction, and she had seen it early on, and she had tried not to see it, tried also to do what she could to bring him back, but he was off, and there was no stopping him, and eventually he did what he did, and left when he left, early, because we were all leaving and he knew that more clearly than other people did, and he was not heartless enough to see the point in trying to stay.

They spoke and were quiet and spoke again, and outside it was cloudy and grew light gradually, and Oona felt a degree of desire in her, and in him, and she rested her palm on his sternum, and they observed one

another, a sort of dimness mixed in with their responsiveness, arousal shadowed by gloom, a feeling not in
keeping with a feeling, and only after a while as Anders announced he was hungry did it occur to Oona
that she was too.

Anders prepared breakfast and Oona took pleasure
in watching him cook, the studious, planned manner
in which he did it, bringing out all the eggs, the salt,
the butter, the vegetables, apparently following a
checklist in his mind, very particular, and she noticed
that when she spoke to him, he stopped what he was
doing and listened, as though he could not do two
things at the same time, and perhaps he could not
do things at the same time, perhaps that was how he
was built, for when he read, he read with such focus,
and when he cooked, he cooked with such focus, and
when he spoke, or he kissed, or he laughed, he was so
relaxed, but when he worked, it seemed to require so
much effort from him, and she wondered how his mind
operated, and what it was to be him, and she almost
expected the omelets he made to taste different, to
taste of his method, his approach, to taste Anders-like,

in some way, as his body tasted Anders-like, but they did not, they were just omelets, and they were pretty good.

───

Oona was at work the evening the riots began, and her class was half-empty, because the riots were predict-able, were in fact rumored, even threatened, and so people were staying home, but something can be both predictable and shocking when it happens, and there was panic in the air as Oona and her colleagues rushed to lock up the studio and get out, and once on the street they could hear it in the distance, the sound of anarchy, or revolution, and Oona could smell it, a smoky smell, and a dark woman and a light man ran by her, with their two children, possibly cut off from their car, and Oona wondered if the woman had al-ways been dark, or if the woman had changed, Oona had not seen the children clearly enough to tell if they looked like the woman, like they could have come from the woman, as she was now, and all this hap-pened in an instant, and then Oona thought to call out, to say her car was right here, and she, Oona, could give them a ride, but by then it was too late, and they were already gone around the corner, and Oona said, hey, said it regardless, not loudly, raising a hand, a hand they would not notice, and why she did this she could not have explained, whether to help them, or to be the sort of person who would have helped them, and one of Oona's colleagues said to Oona, come on come on, and urged her forward, and Oona got into her car and drove off.

Some people seemed to be flowing towards the center of town, from where the riot was spreading, and others were flowing away, but there were not too many of either, and there was a charged feeling all about, and Oona observed that no one was stopping at the stop signs, nor at the traffic lights, and so she did not stop either, though she did slow, and look both ways, and Oona expected to hear sirens, from police cars and fire trucks and ambulances, but she did not hear them, and that was strange, she could hear only one siren, lonesome, far away, as if all the other vehicles with sirens had gone in the wrong direction, or been trapped in their driveways and parking lots, or incinerated, and once she did not hear the sirens, she kept listening for them, kept listening the entire way home, and not hearing them made it worse somehow, made her feel like this was outside the control of human beings, of society, a tidal wave that would come and sweep over town, sweep over every neighborhood, no matter what anyone tried or did.

Her own street was quiet. Peaceful. She parked and went inside, and for a second or two it was as though the whole thing was in her imagination, but in that time she had pulled out her phone and she looked at what it showed, and people were filming what was happening, and the images were images from another world, or at least another country, images of fire and beatings and throngs, jittery angles in excited or terrified hands, and the sounds were of shouts and roars and laughter and screams, and it was impossible to make sense of it, or even to tell if this was here, today, and she had several missed calls from Anders, she had called him without luck from the studio, and he had repeatedly called her back, most recently minutes ago, and she did not know how she could have failed to have noticed, maybe her ringer was on mute or too low, but she dialed him now and it neither rang nor went to voice mail, the line was silent, searching for a connection, even though she had a connection, her signal was full, yet her phone required some technological feedback, was stuck in some limbo, insisting on a prompt that was not forthcoming, permission, a sign of what it should do next, waiting and waiting though the waiting was over.

Eight

The first bitterly cold day of the year arrived, and the deciduous trees were already nearly naked, and that moonless night, alone at home, Anders thought he could feel the ancient horrors awakening, could feel the almost forgotten savagery upon which his town was founded, all of it gathering outdoors, pulling on his windows with the breeze.

He was envious of the militants, just then, in a way, and he wondered, if they had been willing to accept him, whether he would have chosen to be one of them, and part of him suspected it was not entirely impossible that he might have chosen to, eventually, and if he had still been white maybe he would have been out there, blowing pale breath into his hands, secure in his righteousness, or at least safe from their righteousness, but as it was, the choice was not open to him, and he was here, less chilly but more afraid.

The gym had been damaged by fire, not heavily, just a bit, and like most business owners Anders's boss had decided to shut down for a while, and Anders was not let go, but he was not exactly employed either, not in the sense of currently getting paid, and so he had to make do with his savings and what his father had given him, and as he counted his cash and tallied up his supplies that night, he thought suddenly of the cleaning guy, and whether he should call him, and see if he was safe, or whether that was crazy, not Anders's place, but Anders did not have his number, and in any case he realized, surprised, that he did not even know his last name.

Oona messaged, and they spoke until late, and after that Anders wandered online, and in town it seemed people were continuing to change, white people becoming dark, and though the riots had subsided the militants were growing ever more aggressive, and bodies were turning up in fields, commentators disagreeing and arguing as to the exact count, was it two this time or three or six, but no one saying there were none, and people buried them, and the bodies were rumored to be dark, but not exclusively dark, and among the dark ones some who had not always been so.

Anders no longer strayed far from his rifle. He did not venture out, and he slept with it on the floor next to his bed, and he cooked with it propped up against the wall between his refrigerator and a cupboard, and for a while he took it with him to the bathroom, and once this came to seem excessive to him, he simply placed it on the coffee table in front of his sofa, where he could see it, so even then, with the bathroom door open, it was present.

The rifle, though it was meant to make Anders feel secure, also murmured to Anders a quiet but insistent question, which was how much did he want to live, and he could not deny in the interminable afternoons and in the late tree-swaying nights hearing the rifle's question, and he knew that it would be straightforward to end himself, and maybe that was the point, the point of it was to break him, to break all of them, all of us, yes us, how strange to be forced into such an us, and Anders wondered what was happening to other dark people, and how they were coping, and whether they were killing themselves, fast with guns and slow with drinks and pipes and pills, or hanging on, and he did not consider himself a particularly violent man, nor well suited to these times, and his mother was gone, and his father would soon be too, and with them the people he would betray most by leaving, and so if he stayed it would not be for them, need not be for them, but for himself, and yet each day he did stay, bored and tense, true, but he stayed, and he discovered thereby how badly he wanted to stay, that the impulse to live was in him stronger than he might have imagined, undiminished by his bleak circumstances, and by the odd wrapper he was wrapped in, and maybe it was stubbornness, or selfishness, or hope, or fear, and maybe it was desire, the desire to continue to be Anders, or to be with Oona, especially to be with Oona, but whatever it was, it was there, fierce, and so he dressed as warmly as he could, and kept himself fed, and he read and he exercised and waited in his brown skin through those solitary days for what would come next.

After the riots, Oona argued with her mother, berated her mother, talked to her mother, even screamed at her mother, but could not convince her mother, at best she could only unsettle her, and take away part of the happiness her mother was holding on to, and when they fought Oona's mother got angry, but only briefly, more often she became unsteady, and then Oona could glimpse that panic in her eyes, a deep, abiding panic, like an ocean, a panic Oona recognized because that panic was in herself too, and Oona took no pleasure in revealing this within her mother, the opposite in fact, she wanted to hide it, to recoil from it, because of what it revealed in herself, and in many ways it was intolerable for her mother to believe what she believed and behave as she behaved, but in many ways it was better too, much better, than what seemed to be the utter desolation of its alternative, which was to be drowning and to have no belief at all.

Oona's mother resisted the notion that violence was happening, or that substantial violence was happening, and said that if there was violence it was because there were paid aggressors on the other side, saboteurs, and that they were trying to kill both our defenders and our people in general, and they were sometimes killing their own kind, to make us look bad, and also because some of their own kind supported us, and they killed them for that, and that the main point was separation, it was not that we were better than them, although we were better than them, how could you deny it, but that we needed our own places, where we could take care of our own, because our people were in trouble, so many of us in trouble, and the dark people could have their own places, and there they could do their own dark things, or whatever, and we would not stop them, but we would not participate in our own eradication, that had to end, and now there was no time to wait, now they were converting us, and lowering us, and that was a sign, a sign that if we did not act in this moment there would be no more moments left and we would be gone.

Oona could not dispute that her mother did indeed seem improved, that the changes in town, and all over the country, were suiting her mother, in some sense, and Oona had the nagging feeling that her mother was right, not morally, but along a different dimension, that her understanding of the situation was deeper than Oona's was, as though she had access to a mystical truth, a terrible mystical truth, a kind of conjuring that Oona did not believe in and yet that worked anyway, and it was as if all the ghosts were coming back, ghosts coming to each town and each house, ghosts coming to her mother, and compensating her for her loss, and others for their losses, but Oona did not feel compensated, she felt even more bereft.

Oona missed her father after these conversations, her father who was so reliable, who could talk sense into anyone, and she was certain her father could have helped her mother now, or rather that with him still there her mother would not be where she was now, none of them would, but as she thought of her father she wondered if, entirely, completely, he would have disapproved of what her mother was saying, he was not a bad man, not at all, but he was not a saint either, and he did have certain impulses relating to the color of people's skin, which to be fair were common, especially when he had been young, and life had never pushed him into any extremes, he had done well, but if he had not, who could say, and as she pondered it, her ability to see him wobbled a bit, to see who he was, and yet she missed him, her father, and she missed her brother, who had been her father's favorite, and who had missed him so much, too much, her brother who had thought their father walked on water, her brother who would have said to her just then that everything would be fine, who always said that, and was always wrong, and still always said it, whether he believed it or not, hollow, and endearing, and heartbreaking, and maybe her brother was right to go, had been right to go, to start to go as soon as their father had gone, maybe they both had been right, the two men of her family, maybe they had seen what would be coming, and wanted no part of it, and Oona could not blame them for that, should not, but did, and there was no escape, it was up to her.

⸻

Anders had heard that the militants had begun to clear people out, dark people, running them out of town, and when he saw cars pull up to his house he knew what it meant, though it is perhaps always a surprise when what one is waiting for, what one is dreading, a calamity of this magnitude, actually happens, so Anders was prepared and not prepared, but prepared as he was, he was not expecting one of the three men who came for him to be a man he knew, a man he was acquainted with, it made it much worse, more intimate, like being shushed as you were strangled, and Anders did not pause for them to get to his door, Anders opened it himself, and he stood there in the doorway, his rifle in his hands, a ready carry, with muzzle high, the son an echo of his father on a hunt.

Anders hoped he looked more brave than he felt, and the three of them were armed but they stopped when they saw him, a few paces away, and they stared at him with contempt and fascination, and Anders thought the one he knew stared at him with enthusiasm too, like this was special for him, personal, and Anders could perceive how self-righteous they were, how certain that he, Anders, was in the wrong, that he was the bandit here, trying to rob them, they who had been robbed already and had nothing left, just their whiteness, the worth of it, and they would not let him take that, not him nor anyone else.

But they did not particularly relish that he had a

weapon and seemed to have grabbed part of the initiative, that was their role after all, and they were not expecting this from him, and it muddied the simplicity of the situation, and so they halted, and they faced off, his acquaintance, the two strangers, and Anders, and Anders said hello guys, what can I do.

They spoke, and Anders listened, and in the end the men said he had better be gone when they got back, and Anders said they would have to see about that, and as Anders said it he almost believed he would stay, and he had an anger in his voice, an anger he was glad for, despite their dismissive smiles, but when they withdrew to their cars and Anders felt the magnitude of his relief, a relief that washed over him and drenched him with defeat, he knew that he would be gone, that, mere minutes hence, he would be fleeing, and this place, his place, so familiar, would be lost to him, his no longer.

Nine

When Anders arrived at his father's house, his father took him inside and drew the tattered curtains, and then parked his son's car, the car that had been his wife's car, behind the house, on the narrow sliver of land that his wife had called her garden, where once grew flowers and tomatoes and snap peas and thyme, but which now was a patch of dirt with tufts of weeds, weeds dry and dead at the onset of winter, and Anders's father checked to make sure the car was not visible from the street, moving weakly and stiffly, but also with purpose, and after that, spent beyond reckoning, he sat himself next to his son in the living room, the television on and their rifles at their sides, and they

waited there for someone to show up and demand Anders be given over, but no one did, no one came, no,
not on that first night at least.

Anders's father was not yet used to Anders, to how
Anders looked, and in a sense he had never been used
to him, not even when Anders was a child, silent for
so long, struggling to tie his laces or to write in a hand-
writing that people could read, for Anders's father,
while not a particularly good student, had always been
competent, competent at the tasks he was given, and
not just in school, outside it, too, but his son, his son
was different, a difference the boy's mother took to
naturally, and so the boy became her boy, and there
were walls between them, between him and his son,
and Anders's father could understand the bullies who
had picked on his son when his son was small, and he
could understand those who wanted him gone from
town now, who were afraid of him, or threatened by
him, by the dark man his boy had become, and they
had a right to be, he would have felt the same in their
shoes, he liked it no better than they did, and he could
see the end his boy signaled, the end of things, he was

not blind, but they would not take his boy, not easily, not from him, the boy's father, and whatever Anders was, whatever his skin was, he was still his father's son, and still his mother's son, and he came first, before any other allegiance, he was what truly mattered, and Anders's father was ready to do right by his son, it was a duty that meant more to him than life, and he wished he had more life in him, but he would do what he could with what little life he had.

In the morning the power went out, and the house was gloomy with the curtains drawn and no lights, but still there was illumination enough to see by, and Anders's father judged it best they save their candles for nightfall, and so they managed, in the dimness, with Anders speaking to Oona on the phone, learning her electricity had gone too, the two of them talking until they realized they had no way to recharge their devices, they had already used much of what they had, driven their percentages low, and must stop, immediately, and soon after they hung up Anders discovered he no longer had a signal, and neither did his father, and Anders wondered if the service had been cut off intentionally or if the backup batteries at the cell towers had died.

Anders was alone, lying propped up on his old childhood bed, far more alone without access to the online world, or if not literally more alone, then more alone in how he felt, and yes the chatter online had been grim, not just in town but all over the country, but it had been something, and now it was taken from him, and time itself slowed, unwinding, like the minutes were tired, were reaching the finish, and then around midnight the power returned without warning and his phone caught a signal and time spooled back up again and continued.

Days passed, and although they heard the crack of gunfire on occasion, one night right outside, they were not themselves confronted, and Anders should have been relieved to have escaped the militants, temporarily, but if he was, it was a fraught relief, for living again in close proximity to his father, he was shocked to discover the degree of physical pain his father was enduring, pain his father could mask for a beat or two, but not for an entire evening, not for hours at a stretch, and Anders could see it in his father's face, and in his movements, and while his father tried to spare him, and retired to his bedroom often, Anders could hear his muffled grunts and his low-pitched swearing, the battle being waged inside, the battle his father was losing, and it made Anders guilty for not being a better son, for having left his father so abandoned, even if he knew his father would not have permitted it to be otherwise, that just by being here, Anders was taking something from his father, taking his dignity, and forcing his father to allow himself to be seen as he would not, and did not, wish to be seen.

In town sporadic bursts of violence persisted, but people continued to change, more and more, no matter what anyone did, and Oona could discern the effort it was beginning to require for her mother to maintain her optimism, her insistence that all would be sorted out, that they, her mother's side, were winning, and as doubt began to appear in her mother, something else began to appear in Oona, not hope exactly, something less than hope, or a precursor to hope, which is to say a possibility, a possibility of what, she did not know, but a possibility that was not numbness, that cut through numbness, and suggested life.

Oona logged on to her social media accounts, which she usually left untouched, and ignored the clamor, and instead wound her way back through time, to the past summer, and to the summer before that, a less bereaved summer, and to summers even further back, and she selected the pictures of her in which she was at her most tan, her most dark, and often with hair that had been reshaped by the water, by pools and lakes or a beach, hair that was fuller and wilder, and she began to play with these pictures, to darken them further, but this darkened everything, and she wanted only to darken herself, and so she found online the ability to do just that, and fed her images into the algorithm, and witnessed herself transform, and she could alter not just the color of her skin but whatever she wished, and sometimes the result was strange, and sometimes it was striking, beautiful even, and she liked that it was her and not her, and that it was a less recent her, and a less shattered her, a her full of potential, a future her born from a past her, skipping entirely where she was now, not entangled in where she was now, free, and it gave Oona an idea, an idea she could not shake, and did not want to shake, an idea that took her to placing an order, intrigued by what could be.

Oona and her mother avoided going out, unless it was absolutely necessary, for the streets were not safe, not even in their part of town, not even for those who looked like them, because anyone could get caught up in things, some of the violence was just theft, or retribution, or random, and whether reports were exaggerated or not, both Oona and her mother knew firsthand people who had been affected, stories that could not be shrugged off, and so they stayed home.

But deliveries continued, and you could get a pizza or alcohol or medicine or drugs, or anything you might imagine, right there on your doorstep, maybe not in minutes, but certainly in hours, and when her delivery arrived, the delivery guys operating in pairs, one in the car, watchful, the other outside ringing the bell, armed, a pistol on his hip, cap wedged low, pale hair peeking out beyond it, Oona called out to him from her upstairs window and let him see the color of her face and dropped a tip in an envelope and bid him leave the bag where he stood.

He scrutinized the house and did not immediately respond, and Oona stepped away and out of sight like it was all agreed and done, but the car did not move for a minute, a long minute, and then it did, and Oona waited until they were well gone, and she fetched her order, quick out and quick in again, double-locking, and returned to her room, and it was all there, all she had paid for.

Oona applied the makeup with care, painting herself slowly, undoing and redoing when she made an error, and she felt the liquid of the tubes spread until almost dry, until virtually solid, and the powder on the brushes conversely spread like liquid, and she stared at her work with enormous concentration, creating what she might have been embarrassed to create before, been mortified to be seen creating, but what now felt essential to reveal, and the dark woman that emerged, dark and dashing, there was no other word for it, dashing, this woman was absurd, and an affront, and thrilling, and Oona had not meant to keep this face on, this face she had made, she had only wanted to see it, to climb the wall of the canyon, not to settle there on the rim, but she could not resist wearing it for a while, wearing it downstairs and to dinner.

Oona's mother was startled, and then stony in response, saying you should be ashamed of yourself, and when Oona said, I am ashamed of myself, her mother said, oh no you're not but you should be, and Oona said, I am in fact, and then they did not speak again, and ate in silence, and Oona suddenly realized as the silence grew that she had thought she might enjoy this, she had thought a victory of some sort might be hers, but she did not enjoy it, of course she did not enjoy it, and there was no victory for her here, there was only defeat, defeat for them both, and neither could win, or at least she, Oona, could not win, because in her winning was a losing that made it impossible to win, and she went up to her room after, and tried again to see what had excited her in the face she had made, in the face she had made on top of the face her mother had made, her mother and her father, but she could not see it, and the removal was slow and messy, messier than she was familiar with, because she had never been one to use heavy makeup, was unskilled in its ways, and the brown sediment that came off her skin and went in the trash and flowed down the sink felt like the death of a river, like the sterilization of a river in a lab.

Ten

Online you could form your own opinion of what was going on and your opinion was, likely as not, different from the next person's, and there was no real way to determine which of you was right, and the boundary between what was in your mind and what was in the world beyond was blurry, so blurry there was almost no boundary at all.

For Anders the images that stuck with him most were of two men in town, two dark men, meeting not far from Anders's place, the place he had fled, and it seemed they might have known each other, but it was hard to tell, because at first they approached like they did know each other, but when they got closer it seemed they did not, and their words were inaudible, the only sounds were sounds from the man filming them, inside his house, filming them outside on the street, some distance away, his reasons for doing so unclear, and then, without warning, one of the two dark men ducked, ducked like a boxer dodging a punch, but without that grace, that control, kind of clumsily, and as he went down, the other one pulled out a gun, and as he came back up again, the other one shot him casually in the head, casually, and he ducked again, but this time he was not ducking, he was falling, and the words in the video, oh shit oh shit, said almost excitedly, suggested this was in part entertaining, and then the shooter walked away and the other man lay there and did not move, and the video went on for a good minute more, and he did not move, or if he moved, it was not enough to be visible, and Anders could not stop wondering if he knew one of the two, not that they were recognizable, they were not, not to Anders, but one or both might have changed, and there was something about them that was familiar, the way they stood, maybe, or maybe one of them looked like Anders looked now, looked almost like he could be a sibling to Anders, to what Anders had become, and Anders had never had a sibling, and so it was a strange feeling, the feeling that the shooter was related to him, though how he was related, Anders could not have said.

There had been other killings in town caught on camera, but this killing captured the imagination, and people were commenting on it, the killing itself was at the center of an online brawl, a brawl over its meaning, what had happened there, what it meant, and Anders had no idea what it meant, but it seemed it meant something, and he watched it again and again, and he did not leave his father's house, not even for a moment.

Oona had seen the same video when it had surfaced a couple weeks before, but it had receded from her imagination quickly, and instead she found herself noticing the ways in which life in town was going back to normal, or if not going back to normal, at least stopping becoming increasingly abnormal, with more people changing, so many it was almost to be expected when the next one did, it was commonplace, it seemed that half her online contacts had changed, and that there was less violence on the streets, less violence being reported, and one or two people she knew, the most daring among her acquaintances, were starting to go out again, to go for drives, seeing what was up, at least in the daytime, filming from behind their steering wheels or in their passenger seats, and Oona, seeing them, and seeing this, started to feel the desire to go out herself, not just yet, maybe not just yet, but if things continued like this, then soon.

Though by this point several of them had surely changed color too, Anders still wondered if the neighbors could be trusted, and it was not that they were new to him, most had been neighbors forever, but maybe he was new to them, darkened as he was, and not an Anders they had any loyalty to, not an Anders they considered Anders, and it left him uneasy that his car was parked behind the house, where the neighbors could observe it, but an old vehicle was no clear evidence, not of him, not by itself, certainly not if you had no other reason to suspect, and it would have left him more uneasy to have parked the car anywhere else, it offered, in the end, a kind of freedom, an option to flee, and Anders had asked his father when he first arrived what his father thought about the matter, whether the neighbors might find out and turn him in, but his father had refused to answer, or maybe he had answered, come to think of it, for a while later, he had said, you had best avoid the windows, and probably that was his take on that, and Anders, well, Anders had pressed him no further.

Being stuck indoors exacted its toll, and though it was cold out, on some days the sun blazed too, a bright clean winter's sun, the kind that left you snow-blind if your eyes were bare and there was snow on the ground, and with the curtains drawn Anders could make out only slivers of it, cracks of light and vertically sliced sightings of the world beyond, up and down and narrow, sightings shaped like the bars of a cell, and he felt imprisoned, doubly, triply imprisoned, in his skin, in this house, in his town.

He told Oona not to come but eventually she came anyway, saying things were getting better, and people were adjusting now, and those militants that were left would not bother her, though this last part she was unsure of, and there was more than relief in Anders when Oona visited, relief was too tame a word, and Anders's father retired when she joined them, greeted Oona and spoke to her for a minute and then retired to his bedroom, and there was relief for Oona too in finally coming, and also something juvenile about the situation, as though they were kids in school again, and by this time Anders was out of pot, and in any case he never smoked around his father, his father eternally opposed to weed while having no problem with tobacco, which his father consumed in copious amounts, his butts neatly ground out in ashtrays, the smell permeating every fabric in the house, and Oona still had a weed supply, one of her sources had vanished, but she had another, and would have brought some had Anders not forbidden it, since sneaking out to smoke, as he had done throughout his teens, was now too risky to contemplate, and without weed they talked and listened to music and sat on the sofa, and the first time they kissed in the house, Anders's father, headed to the kitchen, glimpsed them and immediately looked away, and Oona thought he was being considerate, but Anders saw something else, he saw the discomfort on his father's face, the discomfort at seeing this white girl kiss this dark man, even though the dark man was not a dark man, even though the dark man was Anders, and Anders told himself he was mistaken, told himself he was mistaken when he knew he was not mistaken, and his father was not a discreet person, but he did do his best not to show it, not to reveal to his son that Anders was anything other than Anders, less than Anders, and for Anders his father doing his best was all there was or could be, and it would of course have to do.

———

Oona's mother could not help but notice the dark faces on her street, more it seemed every day, maybe not wandering around, not that bold, not yet, but playing briefly on their lawns when their lawns were dusted with snow and stepping out in the early hours to shovel their walks, one even waving to Oona's mother when she caught her eye, as though it was all perfectly natural, and nothing had changed, but it was not natural, and everything had changed, even if no one seemed able to see that but her.

The television channel she watched most had gone

off the air, but now was back, and there were dark hosts mixed in with the white hosts, and they were awkward with each other, awkward and unnatural, and they joked even as they discussed circumstances that were bleak, and one of her favorite radio person-alities had changed color, and changed brains it felt like too, and what he said now made no sense, as if he was an impostor, a fraud, and Oona's mother could stand to listen to him no longer.

Online the conversation had moved on to the search for a cure, and while some were trying to re-treat, to find places unaffected, convinced the calam-ity was infectious, and talked about islands and hills and forests far away, Oona's mother could not go, and most others could not either, and so the general buzz was about progress towards discovering a way to undo the horror, but for every story of a miracle drug or concoction that made you white again, there were three or four of someone who had grown terribly sick from imbibing it, or had even died, and Oona's mother was losing hope.

One night a mighty explosion went off in town,

and the shock wave passed right through her house, rattling the windows, more than rattling them, testing them, it seemed, to their limits, and passing through her too, through her organs, and after an instant of fear, Oona's mother felt a little thrill, felt that something was happening, something big, maybe the tide was shifting, maybe at last real heroes had come, but then Oona entered her bedroom and said, wow did you hear that, and Oona's mother said, I did, and Oona said, it's quite a storm, and raised the blinds, and Oona's mother saw the lightning and the sleet coming down and the naked trees, illuminated by the flashes, and she heard the thunder, not so strong anymore, and she started to cry.

Oona climbed into bed with her mother, as she had not in weeks, or possibly in a lifetime, and she held her mother, and cradled her, like a small child hugging a full-grown parent, that was the difference in size, but not like that either, instead like the opposite, a giant child hugging a tiny parent, reborn into another life, in reverse order, a life where none of the old rules any longer applied.

Eleven

Anders's father rarely left his bedroom now, and there was a smell in it, a smell he could see in Anders's face when his son entered, and sometimes could even smell himself, which was strange, like a fish feeling it was wet, and the smell they could smell was the smell of death, which Anders's father knew was close, and this frightened him, but he was not completely afraid of being frightened, no, he had lived with fear a long time, and he had not let fear master him, not yet, and he would try to continue, to continue to not let fear master him, and often he did not have the energy to think, but when he did, he thought of what made a death a good death, and his sense was that a good death would be one that did not scare his boy, that a father's duty was not to avoid dying in front of his son, this a father could not control, but rather that if a father did have to die in front of his son, he ought to die as well as he was able, to do it in a way that left his son with something, that left his son with the strength to live, and the strength to know that one day he could die well himself, as his father had, and so Anders's father strove to make his final journey to his death into a giving, into a fathering, and it would not be easy, it was not easy, it was almost impossible, but that is what he set his mind, while he had his mind, on attempting to do.

The pain had reached proportions where periodically there was nothing else left, yearlong hours when there was no person, no Anders's father, just the pain, but then the pain receded for a bit and there was a person again, and when he was a person again, Anders's father could look his changed son in the eye, and nod to him, and let the boy take his hand, and listen to the boy's sparse gentle words, so like the words his wife, the boy's mother, had once used, and then, when it was time, gesture with his head to the door so the boy might step away as the pain came to claim his father again.

After weeks there in hiding, Anders finally ventured out of his father's house, ventured out to score medication to blunt some of the edge of his father's agony, learning about a hospice employee known for his shady dealings, and calling him, and the man who answered said Anders would need to come in person if he wanted to talk, and he sounded so white that Anders did not relish revealing his own color, but Anders put his rifle in his car, and mustered his courage, and drove over there, and no one bothered him on the road, and the man who sounded white turned out to be dark, and Anders thought he did not look like his voice, and then he thought, who knows, maybe he thinks the same about me.

Anders explained his situation, and it was unclear if the man believed him, or if he did not, but he advised Anders on what Anders needed, and Anders paid in cash, and there was of course no prescription and no attempt to pretend there was a prescription, there was just a brown paper bag that for some reason reminded Anders of when he was a boy and his father took Anders with him to work and they sat among all the strong men at that building site, and the men respected his father, you could see it in how they acted, and Anders had felt proud as he sat with them, a boy among men, and they had opened their bags and had lunch together like equals.

On the way back to his father with the painkillers, both hands on the steering wheel, Anders noticed just how many dark faces there were, and how the town was a different town now, a town in a different place, a different country, with all these dark people around, more dark people than white people, and it made Anders uneasy, even though he was dark too, but he was reassured to observe that some of the stores had reopened and the traffic lights were mostly working, and he even passed an ambulance and it was just driving normally, no siren blaring, just driving from someplace to someplace on a regular day, in no hurry, how crazy was that, and when he got home he went to his father and gave his father the medication, and then Anders passed from room to room and spread the curtains, he spread the curtains wide.

The nights were still more unnerving than the days, and the first time in months that Anders went out at night, it was late at night, very late, after Oona called him and asked him to come over, and he was about to say she should come over instead, because he did not like the idea of leaving his father, but also he did not like the idea of Oona driving alone at that hour, things were not yet reliably calm, and random violence continued to occur, and probably he should have said let's meet tomorrow, but there was something about the way she spoke, something inviting in the way she spoke, something open, and also when she spoke he realized how desperate he was to get out, to see her elsewhere, in fact to see her home, which he had seen only once before, when they were children, and Anders had gone with some guys to hang out with Oona's brother, one of those guys, Anders later learned, being Oona's brother's boyfriend at the time, and now Anders was Oona's boyfriend, more or less, and he wanted to be in Oona's house with Oona, and when she prompted him for an answer and said well, stretching the word out, well, like there was a spring in the middle, such a long well the way she said it just then, Anders said yes and he was on his way.

It was bitingly cold that night and there were no clouds and the moon was gone, it had been the sharpest of sliver moons when it was there, the thinnest of cuts in the ink of the sky, and that sharp moon had given off little light, and now it was elsewhere, below the horizon, and the night was dark, a deep, abiding dark, and many of the street lamps were dead, and it felt different to Anders as he drove in his car than it did during the day, it felt unresolved, the menace not entirely receded, like the town had a score yet to settle, and this all would not be over until that settling was done, and then Anders told himself to stop it, to stop agitating himself, he told himself to relax, or not to relax but to be calm, to keep his wits about him and watch as he went, and he went and nothing happened and then he was there.

Oona came out to get him and she was whispering so he whispered too and she said her mother was asleep and then she kissed him, a good strong kiss with the full length of her body, and they went inside quietly and she led him upstairs, pointing to one of the steps and shaking her head, so he would not put his weight on it, and then they were in her room, and he heard a gasp but she smiled as though not to worry and whispered, that's just how she sleeps, meaning her mother, and Oona shut the door, and there was something about being in her childhood room, her still partly childlike room, with her mother nearby, that made Oona excited, and Anders excited, and maybe the vague fear of the drive over was part of it, but they were excited for each other and Anders stripped her and she stripped him and they had sex in her small bed and were not aware of much else until it was done.

But when it was done Oona looked at the door and her expression changed and Anders looked at the door and the door was open and in the doorway was Oona's mother and Anders recognized her but she did not recognize Anders, and for a second Anders thought she was going to scream, but she did not scream, instead she ran, or if not ran, she heaved, she heaved herself out of the doorway and down the hall and towards her bathroom and before she could make it her guts heaved too and she could not control them, she doubled over and vomited on the carpet, heaving and heaving with her eyes wet and her nose wet until her stomach was empty and even after that, and Oona was standing beside her, wrapped in a bathrobe, furious and reassuring, somehow both at once, but more furious than reassuring, and Oona did not bend to assist her mother, she only stood there, and the dark man who was Anders was already on his way out, headed to his car, and the sound of it starting came from the street, and then Anders, the smell of Oona still on him, was going, was gone.

When Oona changed there was no pain, and yes there was surprise, but Oona had known it was coming, and was already somewhat perplexed it was this delayed, and so she lay in her bed taking it all in with her heart beating fast but without panic, looking at her arm, touching her skin, feeling her stomach and her legs, and then using her body to stand, and her body worked as it had before, there was no sense of her balance being off, or of her proportions being any different, though she did feel lighter in a way, darker, yes, but also lighter, less weighty, and not thinner, the weight departing not from her flesh but from something else, somewhere else, a weight from outside her, from above her maybe, that she had borne for so long, without being aware of the bearing of it, and now it was gone, as though the mass of the planet had changed subtly, and there was less gravity for people to contend with.

Oona went to the mirror and saw a stranger, but a complete stranger only for an instant, wondrous, that mouth, those eyes, and then a stranger Oona had met, a stranger who was growing familiar, whom Oona greeted with a steady gaze, and who gazed steadily back, until they both smiled the smallest of smiles, Oona and this dark woman together, this dark woman who was so recently a stranger and who was Oona, undeniably Oona, too.

Oona did not know where it came from, but a feeling of melancholy touched her then, a sadness at the losing of something, and perhaps it was her attachment to the old Oona she was mourning, to the face she had known and the person she had been, the person she had lived within and appeared as, or if it was not that, then perhaps it was an attachment to certain memories that she had evoked in herself, to memories she presently wondered whether she would continue to evoke, an attachment to a person connected to that person who had been a little girl once, and who had not yet lost her father and her brother, and who had not yet had to struggle to keep from losing her mother, but of course the people she had been previously themselves looked different, they looked different from how she, Oona, had looked only yesterday, she had changed before she had changed, she had changed every decade and every year and every day, and so she thought there was no reason that she must lose her memories, the ones she wished to keep.

And in any case the melancholy was fleeting, at least it was fleeting that morning, for the lightness was stronger than the melancholy, the sense that she was escaping a prison she desired to escape, for her life had become fraught, and for so long there had been no way out, there had been that feeling, the feeling that there was no way out, but now it seemed that there might be a way out, that she could shed her skin as a snake sheds its skin, not violently, not even coldly, but rather to abandon the confinement of the past, and, unfettered, again, to grow.

PART
THREE

Twelve

When Oona's mother saw Oona she knew it was Oona, and Oona's mother sat on her sofa and did not speak, and then Oona said, mother, and her mother looked down, still at Oona, but at Oona's legs, at the jeans her daughter was wearing, jeans Oona had had a long time, and then at Oona's running shoes, bright shoes Oona had bought this past autumn, and not at Oona's face, her daughter's face that was brand new, and Oona said, I'm sorry, and why Oona said it she did not know, and her mother was silent for a moment, and for another moment too, but after those moments her mother was not silent, and her mother said, maybe we should have breakfast, and somehow this felt to Oona like the very best thing, the very best thing her mother could possibly have said, and if it did not feel like that, Oona forced it to feel like that, and Oona smiled and nodded and said, yes it's on its way.

In the kitchen Oona busied herself with the plates and the stove and the fridge and a knife. Fruit had been hard to come by lately but they had bright purple beets that were fresh and Oona peeled and diced them with potatoes and set both to boil and then browned them in a skillet with onions and two pairs of eggs and when she was done their breakfast was tasty and colorful and had that sweetness her mother liked, and even though it was not much, it was not ordinary either.

Oona's mother watched her meal as she ate and did not really talk, but she said, it's good, and that was plenty for Oona, and at one point Oona caught her own reflection in an unused serving spoon, a reflection bent and misshapen and dull, but noticeable for being dark, noticeable for the too-small dark head compressed in the concavity, darker somehow than the hand that was holding it by the stem, and Oona scraped that clean spoon around in the last of the food in the skillet and the reflection vanished and the spoon became a spoon again and not some funhouse mirror.

Oona's mother sat there and put her breakfast in her mouth, one bite at a time, and she kept chewing and swallowing, though her mouth grew dry and her jaw felt tired and the swallowing became harder and harder to do, and Oona's mother knew this must be difficult for Oona, so difficult for her poor, once-beautiful daughter, to be like that now, look like that now, that, to have everything taken from her, and she, Oona's mother, was of course a good person, a good, good person, and she wanted to be supportive of her daughter, and she did her very best to keep it all inside her, and to stay at that table, but it was a struggle, an impossible struggle, and when her will failed her she stopped, stopped eating, stopped even chewing, and left what little was left on her plate, and pushed her chair back, and stood and climbed the stairs to her room and spat the pasty residue that was still in her mouth into the sink and turned on the tap and washed it down, pushing it through the small gaps in the drain when it got stuck, and she said to herself in her mind, you can do this, you can do this, but she could not do it right now, and she shut her bedroom door and did not go out again that morning.

Oona waited for her mother to return though she knew her mother would not return and her waiting was like a vigil, but vigils have a duration, they do not last forever, and after a while Oona got up and cleared the table and tidied the kitchen and washed the dishes and scrubbed them clean and her fingers were wrinkled when she was done and they did not look drained of blood, the way they used to after washing, emptied from the inside, they looked gray, like chalk had been dusted on them, or like salt had come up from within waterlogged soil, and Oona took some cream and she rubbed and rubbed her fingers, rubbed and rubbed them until they were supple and glowing again, the brown rich and restored to its vitality.

Oona arrived at Anders's father's house and Anders came out to get her, and Oona half raised her arms, palms up, as if to say, so this is me, and Anders stared at her, and he said, wow, and he shook his head, and she kissed him then and the kiss felt different because her lips felt different, or his lips felt different on her different lips, and she apologized to him for what had happened, and he made a squished gesture with his mouth and said a small thanks, and she saw the sadness in his eyes and she realized that he did not think that she was apologizing for her mother, for her mother's behavior the other night, which she was, but rather that she was condoling with him about his father, and when she went inside and observed how bad it was, she understood she had arrived at the very end of Anders's time in this life as a son to a parent and really nothing else mattered for Anders then but that.

Oona held Anders's hand, and with his other hand Anders held his father's hand, and as they sat and lay there, the three of them connected in a kind of chain, Oona would have liked to speak to Anders's father, and to have asked him about his son when his son was a boy, and about his son's mother, and about himself, about him as a young man when he was not yet Anders's father, but the moments of conversation were past now, at least they were past for Oona and Anders's father, and now there was just the company and the wait.

For Anders, though, there would be moments when his father spoke in his last days, just a word here or there, or occasionally the shortest of sentences, and Anders was glad for these moments, these words, even though he did not always understand them, for his father no longer spoke as clearly as he once did, and around then, when words were said that were no more than sounds, Anders often sensed his mother, or anyway Anders sensed his memories and his missing of her, and he hoped his father sensed his mother as well.

Anders's father sometimes looked at the dark person sat at his bedside and knew it was his son, but sometimes he looked at Anders and did not know who he was, but he knew that he had a duty to this person, that he ought to give him what he could, and so he tried to, and did his very best, even, or especially, when he was unsure who this person was, because then he felt a father feeling, or maybe it was a son feeling, as though he was the son and this person was the father, both of them father, both of them son, and they had a bond, and they would make the passage together, or if not together, at least they would approach it not unaccompanied.

Almost everybody in town had changed by now and there were just stragglers left, pale people who wandered like ghosts, like they did not belong, except that these ghosts grasped that their days were numbered, and so they were haunted more than haunting, and people looked at them as they transited, and they sometimes could not sleep, because they did not know what would happen when they slept, more so than usual, which was only to be expected, for even under normal circumstances falling asleep can seem impossible when one is awake, and then it is happening, and not a matter of possibility, but a living dream, inhabited, and though impossible, already begun.

Most of the shops and offices and restaurants and bars reopened, and most of the gas stations too, and damage was repaired, and shattered glass was swept up and burn marks were plastered and painted over, other than in places where the owners were gone, where they had died or run away, those places staying as they were, and then decaying, reminders of what had happened here, stark accusations, cracks in the floor of a town that suggested problems buried in the foundation.

Anders went to see his boss at the gym and his boss was very dark, and still very big, bigger possibly, although it could have been the color, and there was something wounded about his boss, something maybe broken, but he tried to smile at Anders like it was all a kind of joke, and when Anders told him about Anders's father and said he needed a little time, his boss replied that it was not a problem, and he said words that were not strange, that should not have been strange, but that were strange for him nonetheless, strange for how he had been before, and what he said, almost tentatively, was that he was sorry for the old man and for Anders, and that he wished both of them good luck.

Anders did not recognize anyone else at the gym, and as he drove home he figured it would be a while before people knew who other people were, other than, of course, those who were dark from before, and he wondered if people who had been born dark could tell the difference, could tell who had always been this way and who had become dark only recently, and Anders tried to guess as he drove, basing his guesses on how someone walked, or how they moved, how they appeared, and he did not know if those who seemed most hidden in themselves, their postures turned inwards, their faces shrouded, if that was a dark-person thing, what dark people had long done, or if it was a sign instead of a person who had become dark, and was concealing themselves, as he too had first tried to do, upon changing, or if it was neither, and had always been common, and he was only noticing it now because he was looking.

Oona, too, as she passed around town, and returned to work, went through the process of relearning who was who, or what name belonged to whom, for who you were was not the same as it once had been, and she herself was still Oona but not still Oona, she was changed for having changed, although precisely how she could not say, other than for being better able to tell one dark person from another, for seeing finer gradations in the texture of someone's skin and the shape of their cheekbones and the nature of their hair, like people were suddenly trees, all trees, and no one was anything else, and it was possible to distinguish one from the other by their branches and their bark and their leaves and their height, but not to the extent of one seeming to be a tree and the other seeming to belong to a different category of plant, a moss, say, or a fern.

There was a kind of blindness in seeing people this way, and Oona ran into people she knew without knowing that she knew them, and had a more difficult time judging what sort of person a person was, whether they were nice or friendly or dangerous, but along with this blindness, as with actual blindness, there was a new kind of sight, other senses that grew stronger, a feeling that developed from how someone spoke to her, and how their mouth moved, and what expression their eyes appeared to hold, what light she saw in them, was it curiosity or anger, and she had to work harder to make her way with people, starting from scratch every time, and it was tiring, wearing her out by the end of the day, and she slept more soundly than in a while.

Once Oona was driving and a police car pulled up beside her and the police officer was a woman and she did not resemble a police officer, not in the least, and Oona wondered for a second if the woman had ever resembled a police officer, and then the woman looked at Oona and she had that police officer gaze, the kind of gaze that made Oona fake a smile obediently and look quickly away, and Oona thought to herself, impostor or not, the woman played the role well.

Thirteen

Oona's mother was among the last in town to change, and there was dread in it for her, and also pride, a sense that she had done her best and held on longer than most, though at times she thought conversely that she had done nothing, that there was no reason for her being so late, no sign of success to be found in her lateness, it was just how things were.

She went into Oona's room, and Oona was still sleeping, and when Oona's mother sat on her bed, Oona woke up and was startled, and Oona's mother could see the momentary fear in her daughter's eyes, fear before her daughter understood what was going on, and this pained Oona's mother, for no parent wishes to see their beloved child frightened, least of all by the sight of themselves, but in a way it pleased her a little too, it pleased her a little for her daughter to reveal this fear of a dark stranger, because it felt to Oona's mother like this disarmed her daughter of a weapon and made them closer to being equals, their memories of the fights they had had now more fair.

Oona spent those first days, those first days after her mother turned dark, concerned that her mother could harm herself, for to Oona her mother was broken, and might now be unwilling to stay, and so Oona barely slept for a couple of nights, and kept checking in on her mother, and Oona had resumed work by then, but she took some time off, so she could be home, maintaining a watchful eye, but her mother showed no sign of wanting to end her own life, of preparing to overdose on pills, or slit her wrists in the bathtub, no, Oona's mother seemed, if anything, improved for having changed, or if not improved, then relieved in a way, like someone who was terrified of roller coasters, and who had been pressured by their friends to take one alongside them, and who was disembarking from the ride, shaken and spent, even betrayed, but who was done with it now, and ready to continue, ready to continue with what remained of their late afternoon.

None of which was to say that Oona's mother had an easy time of it, she was stunned for a period, and pensive, and refused to see people, or to be seen by them, other than by Oona, but Oona's mother had been tending towards reclusiveness for quite a while, and had spent the winter confined to her home, and she followed with renewed attention the social media feeds of her acquaintances, all of whom had likewise changed, and some of whom had tentatively begun posting pictures of themselves, their current selves, as though participating in a scandalous town-wide masquerade, but Oona's mother did not herself post any picture, and did not write anything, and looked and looked and looked, but did not yet participate.

Oona wondered whether her mother's collapse would come later, if in a month or two she would plunge into the kind of extinguishing despair Oona had long dreaded would take her, but Oona also wondered the opposite, if her mother had not been quite as broken as Oona had imagined, if her mother was always going to find a way to carry on, and had simply been mourning, or not simply, there was nothing simple about it, but mainly, mainly been mourning, as a woman who had lost her husband and her son was entitled to do, and if it had instead been Oona's fear that had caused her to overestimate her mother's fear, and she did not know, Oona did not know, in retrospect, if things truly had been as precarious as she had imagined them to be, she knew only that they seemed, just possibly, a little less precarious now, and this soothed her somewhat, relaxed her, just a bit, sanded away a small portion of her near-constant edge, and made her, slightly but perceptibly, better able to commit to her sleep when she slept.

One evening Oona saw her mother looking at the social media profile of a dark, handsome couple, a woman and a man with a certain carriage to them, and also a certain sheepishness, the two of them both proud and self-conscious, and her mother kept looking at them, and Oona thought, though she could not be sure, that her mother knew these people, because there was something familiar about them to Oona, despite the fact that, when Oona glanced down at their earlier, paler pictures, she did not recognize them at all.

Anders's father died on a crisp, clear morning, shortly after dawn, and Anders was with him in his room when he passed, for he had noticed the change in his father's breathing that night, and he had stayed there with him, and his father had opened his eyes in the darkness, and he had seen Anders at his bedside, Anders seeing his father seeing Anders, and Anders's father had shut his eyes again, and his already labored breathing had grown more labored, until the effort was palpable, the sound of it filling the room, as though Anders's father was breathing through a cloth that was getting thicker and thicker, and the force required by his lungs was increasing, and when he stopped breathing it was after a mighty breath, a mighty breath that took everything out of him, that took him out of him, and with that breath Anders's father was no more.

Anders did not cry at first, he simply sat, and in sitting it was as if they were waiting for something,

Anders and his father, and the hand in Anders's hand was not yet cold, and it was not until Anders took out his phone, a phone he hated in that moment, hating its profanity, the falseness of the distancing it committed against what felt like a sacred immediacy, it was not until he held that slab of glass and metal and its screen lit up and he sought to operate it one-handedly, or one-thumbedly, really, that he started to cry, and he wept so hard and so loud that it surprised him, and made him want to shush himself, and Oona, who answered, could not understand him, but she understood what had happened, what must have happened, and she was on her way, and soon she was there.

Anders's father had died without debt and having paid for his own funeral arrangements, both being matters of principle for him, severe and uncommon principle, and he had apprised Anders in advance of what had to be done, and the men from the mortuary had arrived like well-dressed plumbers, and they had taken Anders's father to their hearse, and transported him to the funeral home, Anders and Oona following, as though Anders was afraid his father might be stolen or misplaced, and it was only there that Anders was convinced to leave his father, the professionals telling Anders he would be called to see his father again, as soon as his father was readied, and they did this telling well, they had experience of it, but more than that they spoke in a matter-of-fact fashion that was firm without diminishing the enormity of the situation, and Anders listened to them as others before him had listened to them, and did as they said and went home.

On the drive back the sun was shining as though nothing had happened and there was no snow on the ground and there were hints of green here and there and it was a normal day that could have been almost a nice day, a day that suggested, inappropriately, jarringly, that winter would soon be over, and that spring was beginning to be sprung, and it all just hit Anders, unslept and red-eyed, it hit him right in the face.

Anders had been with his father through that time when many fathers would have been in hospital, and because it had been only the two of them at home, Anders's father's dying had been intimate for Anders in a way that Oona's father's dying and Oona's brother's dying had not been for Oona, it had been an older manner of dying, and Anders felt uncomfortable to be separated from his father now, to have others preparing his father for burial, and he kept saying, I should be with him, I should be with him, and Oona did not know what was the right way to reply, but she also knew that it did not matter what one replied, and so she sat with Anders and held Anders and sometimes said to Anders, you will, love, wait, you will.

Oona heard herself saying the word love and it moved her to say it and it pleased her to say it and there was a pleasure mixed in with the sadness of those moments for her, a pleasure in saying that word and knowing it was true, as though she could not have known it without testing it and seeing if it carried her weight and now she had and it did.

Maybe Anders idealized his father and maybe Anders's father was a connection to the distant past for Anders, to traditions with which Anders was not yet familiar and would not now ever be familiar, but Anders was seized with the idea that he should dig his father's grave, dig it himself, and he wondered then if Anders's father had dug Anders's grandfather's grave, and for some reason he thought, he just thought, that he had, and Anders almost called the graveyard and asked if he could, and then he stopped himself and said to himself, this is crazy, and he did not do it, he did not do it even though he could imagine the feel of the grain of the wooden shaft and the heft of that shovel in his hands, biting into the dirt, but he regretted that decision later, he regretted it, not bitterly, no, only faintly, but he regretted it for as long as he lived.

At the service for Anders's father the casket was half-open, reminding Anders of the back door of their house, which was a two-part door, and Anders's father had sometimes stood there when Anders was a boy, the lower part shut, the upper part open, and Anders's father had liked to rest one hand on the edge and to smoke with the other, and he had looked at Anders with that expression Anders could not quite read, not with affection, not exactly, but not without affection either, more like he was trying to figure something out, and Anders's father's eyes were closed now, and he had makeup on now, it made him a little strange, and Anders could not see his expression, and Anders would not see his expression again.

Anders had thought he would hate the funeral service but he did not hate the funeral service, it was comforting to be with these other people who came to offer their respects, and Anders did not know who was who and which was which, not until they introduced themselves, although occasionally he could guess, and there were not many of them, but there were enough, the right number, all those who were present being those who cared, and the ceremony did what it was meant to do, which was to make real what had happened and to weave Anders and those others left behind into a shared web of what they had lost, and Anders's pale father was the only pale person present, the only pale person left in the entire town, for there were by that point no others, and then his casket was closed and his burial was occurring and he was committed to the soil, the last white man, and after that, after him, there were none.

Fourteen

Oona's mother did not speak much, not for weeks, and she stared out the windows, and stared at her hands, and stared at her screens, and on her screens she could not help going back to some of the venues she had frequented before, and some of these venues were gone, or were quiet, but some of them were active, even more active, and on some of the active ones the talk was of the end of the world.

The final chaos was approaching, it was said, a descent into crime and anarchy, and cannibalism, cannibalism out of hunger, and, worse, out of vengeance, and blood would flow, and all should prepare for the end, gather with the like-minded or barricade themselves in their homes, ready for the last stand, the last stand before we were overrun, because we were no safer for being dark, they could tell the difference, they still knew who we were, what we were, and they would come for us now, now that we were blind, and could not see one another, could not see which of us was actually us, and they would come for us like predators in the night, taking their prey when their prey was defenseless.

Oona's mother read of the savagery, the savagery of the dark people, how it had been in them from the beginning, and had manifested itself again and again throughout history, and could not be denied, and she read the examples, the examples of when groups of whites had fallen, and the rapes and slaughters and tortures we had been subjected to, and how that was their way, the way of the dark people, whenever they seized the upper hand, and she was frightened, frightened by what she read, but maybe not as frightened as she had expected to be, or not for as long as she had expected to be, for her daughter came and went from the house on her bicycle, and smiled at Oona's mother whenever she arrived, and the mail was delivered each day, too much mail, with too many bills, and the plants were stirring, and her garden was budding, and some sunny days it was warm enough to open the windows in the early afternoon, and the smell that entered the house was that spring smell, that smell her husband had once called with a wink the smell of the time to frolic.

Oona's mother did not stop visiting those online venues, but slowly she visited them less, because they alarmed her, or not just because they alarmed her but because they alarmed her and she did not wish so much to be alarmed, not anymore, and the contrast between them and the world around her was just too bewildering, and she did not doubt them, their hearts were in the right place, and they knew a great deal, but also she did not reliably enjoy them, and so, without planning it, but with motivation, Oona's mother spent less of her days online, and as for Oona, Oona noticed that her mother started, little by little, to be ready, in the evenings, to speak.

Anders visited the graveyard every weekend, and usually Oona joined him, they went there together when she had spent the night at his place, and they met there when she had not, and once when he arrived and she was on her way he noticed how many birds there were, and then he saw Oona approaching and dismounting from her bike and chaining it to the fence, double-chaining it with a thick chain and a heavy lock, for bikes were, as always, prone to theft, and Oona was walking towards him, somehow taller than she was, her posture the sort of posture that created an illusion of height, not stiff, but rather long and high-chinned, limber and pulled upwards, all at once, like she was ready to dance, or to fly, and he watched her then and he felt fortunate in her, to have Oona nearing him, upright despite all the load she carried, and she waved and he waved back and it was the first time he had felt fortunate in a while.

Anders's mother and father were side by side in the graveyard, occupying adjoining graves, that afternoon in the shade of a nearby tree, a tree that had lost a massive part of its trunk and bore the scar of it, a scar likely home to small creatures, though none could presently be seen scampering or crawling upon it, upon that tree that careened skywards haphazardly, off-balance but rooted and thick at its base.

Other people might be averse to graveyards and seek to avoid them, but Anders and Oona were not typical in that regard, not that they preferred being in that graveyard, exactly, but they felt something there, and lingered there, lingered among the trees and the plants and the graves, among the occasional mourners, for there were usually few, or even none, and Anders and Oona would tarry a while, mostly alone, and they found a bench or a patch of grass, and they sat there, sometimes for hours, and they spoke, or were quiet, and in a way they were at home.

That day they walked around, slowly, lost in thought, glancing at the graves of strangers, every so often reading an inscription aloud, and Anders said to Oona that he had only rarely been to a graveyard before his mother died, in fact, thinking about it now, he could not remember his first time, and Oona said that she could not remember her first time either, but she remembered when her father was buried, the whole family going then, and how her brother had not gone again after that, had refused to go again, and they had not fought much, her brother and she, but there was this once that their mother had wanted to take them, and her brother said no, and Oona did not like it, did not like the way he said it, because he said it so rudely, but not only for that, also because she heard the fear in his rudeness, she heard the terror there, a terror her family had lived with ever since, and Oona had been alarmed by it, by the sound of it in her brother's voice, and she fought with him, a full-on, raging fight, but he did not budge, and in the end he never went, not to that graveyard, not until he was buried himself.

Anders asked her if she wanted to go there now, and she thought about it, whether she wanted to go there now, to the graveyard where her father was buried, and where her brother was buried in the spot that was intended for her mother, but that would not be occupied by her mother, and Oona realized that she would like to go there, not this moment, but a little later, yes, she would like to go there with Anders, before it grew dark, but not in any hurry, they could take their time, she was calm where she was just then, and graveyards were like airports, they were all connected, and she smiled, and asked if he knew what she meant, and he smiled too, and he nodded and said he did.

They walked on, and Anders put his arm around Oona, and he suspected then that maybe there was something different about them, about Oona and him, and he thought that possibly they felt the dead as not everyone felt the dead, that some people hid from the dead, and tried not to think of them, but Anders and Oona did not do this, they felt the dead daily, hourly, as they lived their lives, and their feeling of the dead was important to them, an important part of what made up their particular way of living, and not to be hidden from, for it could not be hidden from, it could not be hidden from at all.

On a subsequent evening, Anders and Oona walked after work along the main streets in the center of town, and in an ice cream parlor there were a couple of children picking flavors with their parents, and the bars were, if not full, no longer deserted, and Anders and Oona stepped into one such establishment, and sat on a pair of high stools, and heard the music, mercifully not too loud, and looked around them in the reddish dimness, just slightly red, and not so very dim, and they ordered whiskeys and tapped their glasses together, not raising them, but sliding them over, glass meeting glass, less with a clink than with a tap, and then each brought their drink to their lips and sipped the golden liquid therein, and the whiskey burned in their mouths and throats, for they were hungry, and also parched, and no longer accustomed.

Neither had been out for a drink in many months, and it was sort of odd to be out now, and no one there at that bar looked entirely comfortable, not the bartender, and not the men huddled in the only occupied booth, and not Anders and Oona, not any of them, not any of these dark people bathed in the bar-colored light, trying to find their footing in a situation so familiar and yet so strange, and Oona, noticing this, wondered whether it was really the case, or whether people simply looked uncomfortable whenever you thought they were uncomfortable, just as they seemed crazy whenever you thought they were crazy, and maybe everyone looked the same as they always did, the same, just dark.

As she thought this and the whiskey settled into her belly, her perspective changed and the others no longer looked so out of place, and neither did Anders, and she too no longer felt weird, they were just people and this was just a bar and these were just drinks and Anders was just speaking, and she listened to him speaking, catching the second half of what he was saying, and it was gone, the difference was gone, and it was a regular night for Oona once more.

They finished their drinks and decided to go to a restaurant for dinner, there was a place she liked nearby, and this place served no meat and served no dishes that pretended to be meat, and the ingredients were always local and changed with the season, and as they walked there Oona realized she did not know if it would be open, if it still existed, but it was, and it did, and the owners were there, two women, and Oona smiled to one and thought she knew who that one was, and the woman smiled back as though she knew who Oona was, and Oona was surprised by this, for how could the woman know, and then she realized the woman was probably doing that to everyone, treating each arrival as an old customer newly returned.

The meal was a pleasure and a welcome sign of normalcy and not too heavy, and they drank only water, water with no ice, and they could feel the whiskey in them, not much but yes present, in their stomachs and in their veins and on their breath, and they enjoyed the tasting of unfamiliar tastes and the feeling of being with other people, for the restaurant was a quarter full, even though it was late, and when they left the moon was out and they strolled for a bit and they were so relaxed on their stroll, relaxed until this man started to follow them, a dark man who slipped into the same pace as them as they walked, and then drew closer, both Anders and Oona aware of him and sensing his approach, and suddenly the man shouted, and Anders and Oona were startled, more than startled, they were shocked, and they whirled to face him, their inhalations quick and Anders's fists up, and the man started to laugh, he bent over and laughed, and he turned, still bent a bit and still chuckling, and walked slowly away.

Fifteen

Oona's mother had expected a reckoning and when that reckoning did not come, when those who had been white were not hunted down and caged or whipped or killed, other than in a handful of cases where the crimes had been particularly egregious and the perpetrators were known and could be found, when no mass settling of scores occurred in those initial weeks after the transformation of the town was complete, she began to relax, and she found that she did not detest being out among people, no different from the others, not visibly different, not obviously identified as being of one tribe rather than of another, and that it was a kind of reprieve, like when she was a child and her teacher knew the whole class had cheated on a test and instead of calling in the principal had merely said the test would be disregarded, the meaning clear but the judgment suspended, and left the matter at that.

Oona's mother did miss it though, she missed being white, but almost more than her own being white, she missed her daughter being white, and she wondered at times if her grandchildren might be white, if there was still a chance for them, but in her heart of hearts she knew they probably would not be, and this saddened her, but not enough for her not to want to have grand-children, a rekindled desire, as she took an interest in her daughter's love life instead.

It was clear her girl was smitten with this boy, An-ders, and Oona's mother wanted to make things right between them, for he had never again come to visit, and Oona had told her that the boy's father had passed away, and so she told her daughter she wanted to go see him, to offer her condolences, and her daughter had phoned him and he had said this would be fine, and so she went and they did not speak of what had happened that night, a night both of them wanted to forget, and Oona's mother had experience in dealing with the dead and so she sat next to him and after some chitchat she took his hand, surprising Oona, and Anders, and maybe herself too, and she told him that when she was a child she had likewise been an only child, and it was not quite as common then, and she remembered the death of her own father, who had gone after her mother had gone, and Oona's mother had not been married yet, and she understood what it was to be young and to sit in the house of the deceased all by yourself, and Anders looked almost like he was going to cry, but he did not cry, instead he smiled, and watching him she saw him gazing at Oona, and Oona had tears in her eyes, her eyes were wet, the tears pooling in them and not falling, and Oona shrugged, and her mother called her over and hugged her then, hugged her wiry daughter to her ample bosom, and Oona grinned, and Oona's mother thought, we three feel like a family.

It was perhaps not appropriate but she was seized with the desire for a picture, and she sat Oona and Anders together, she could not help it, and stood before them, and took a photo, and their expressions were, what were they, calm, like they were secure in each other, and it was a beautiful photo, and even before she had reached home again, riding beside Oona on the way, Oona's mother had posted the picture to her social media account, the first picture she had posted in such a long time, and the screen of her phone was already cooing back at her, registering marks and comments of online approval.

Oona had to renew her driver's license and the clerk there glanced at her image on the plastic card and at her face, not once but twice, and Oona thought he was going to ask her to prove she was who she claimed to be, since there was no way for him really to tell, but he did not do that, instead he peered at her like he was trying to peer into her, and he said, Oona, did not say it so much as ask it, and she said, yes, and he said his name, just his first name, and there was nothing about him that was unchanged but still she recognized him and they hugged, Oona in particular hugging him tight, and he hugged her too, first not quite so hard, but then equally so, and they agreed she would wait so they could have a coffee together and she did and they did.

The clerk had been her brother's big love, and though he and her brother had had a tumultuous relationship, on and off again throughout high school, and though it had ended badly, had ended badly more than once, on more than one occasion, and though he and her brother had drifted apart, he had come to her brother's funeral, standing far from everyone else, and Oona had meant to speak with him, but he had left before she had the chance, and that was only, could it be, months ago, not quite a full year, but it felt like many years, and even if it had not been many years since they had seen one another, it had been many years since they had spoken, but when they began to speak over coffee it was as if no time had passed, as if they were inhabiting parallel lives, lives running on tracks shunted from but nonetheless alongside the old tracks, and while her brother was gone, in their conversation he was almost alive, almost still alive, and Oona was alive, gripped by life at the throat.

The clerk was a beautiful man with delicate brown eyes and big brown hands, and he had been beautiful when he was a boy too, but not this beautiful, and she asked him if he was happy for having changed, and he said his changing color had been only one of several changes he had been through recently, it all flowed together, he had gotten married the week before her brother's funeral, yes married, he repeated to her expression of surprise, his own expression no less surprised, as though he could barely believe it himself, and he was happy in his marriage, and he loved his husband, but her brother was there too, with him, and he would always be there, he knew that now, he had known it at the funeral, he had married and found a love and lost a love and changed color, and which of these was most significant for him he could not say, but probably, probably it was not the color.

She teased him then and she said it suited him, meaning how he looked now, and he said, I know it does, and they laughed, and he said it suits you too, and she said, really, and he said, really, and he added, you looked too hungry before, and she asked, and now

I don't, and he said, and now you don't, and she smiled, and then she smiled again, her smile bigger and bigger.

It was properly spring and the mornings were cool but they were also gorgeous, and Anders had settled into his father's house, his mother's house, and Oona was sort of settling in there with him, spending more and more nights, and helping in the clearing out and fixing up and making over of the place, and she had things in her mother's house too, and had not left it, but her clothing was accruing in the home she shared with Anders, and for his birthday she got Anders a bicycle and in the gorgeous mornings they biked, biked to work together, stopping each day to pick up a coffee before they parted ways.

The insects were returning, most spectacularly, if tentatively, the butterflies, and as they rode they noticed those spaces where butterflies tended to congregate, and one day there was a whole cloud of them around a little flowering bush, and Anders and Oona stopped and watched them for a while, each rider with one foot on the ground, and they did not speak or photograph but just watched them, and the next day, when they rode by, the butterflies were gone, and Anders turned to Oona to comment on this, and as he opened his mouth a bug went in and he made a revolted expression and tried to get it out, spit it out, and Oona slowed beside him, coasting, and laughed.

The woman who prepared their coffees that day was a new woman, and she wore overalls without a shirt underneath, just a bra, though it was not yet hot, and maybe she did this to reveal her tattoos, which danced on her upper arms and shoulders, and the funny thing about her tattoos was that they were almost the same color as her skin, or not the same color but the same darkness, and so they looked more like etchings than tattoos, fine and intricate and textured, nearly but not quite invisible, and Oona wondered if the woman had had them done after she had changed, and Oona did not know, but she thought not, or she liked to think not, she liked to think the woman had had them done before, and had changed into them, had changed towards them, so to speak, though it struck Oona just then that it was possible the woman had never changed at all, and as Oona paid, as Oona paid the woman, Oona said, nice tattoos, and the woman smiled and said, thanks.

It seemed to Anders that his coffee tasted different, but he was unsure whether it actually did, or if this was an aftereffect of the bug in his mouth, and he sipped his coffee without his usual enthusiasm, but when he and Oona kissed goodbye it was a longer and more passionate goodbye kiss than was typical for them in the morning, and it took him by surprise, though not her, as it came from her, and with that, and without a further word, they parted ways, she going to the studio and he to the gym.

In the gym the fire damage had been repaired, and mostly painted over, but still some signs remained, observable here and there, and the months out of operation had taken their toll on the finances of the place, it appeared basic, especially basic against the flowering of spring, no-frills, the bare minimum, benches and racks and barbells and plates and bands and chains, and the mirrors in the main area were dusty, and Anders wondered if the cleaning guy had been told not to clean them so much anymore.

The ranks of lifters who used the gym had been depleted somewhat, maybe because times were hard, or maybe because some of them were gone, but there were a couple of new lifters too, clients who had not been clients before, and in any case the lifting was the same, focused, and desperate, exertions of maximal force, for five repetitions, or three, or one, men pushing themselves as hard as they could push themselves, not exercising, but training, and perhaps not even training, but fighting, fighting the gravity the world exerts on all those who walk upon it, exerts seemingly equally, though in actuality not equally, not equally at all.

Of everyone there, the cleaning guy seemed the least changed, and Anders watched him go about his work, and wanted to strike up a conversation, but none of his attempts really went anywhere, and that day Anders had an idea, and he waited until late, and no one else was nearby, and he said to the cleaning guy, I could train you, you could work out here sometimes, like the rest of us do, would you like that, and the cleaning guy looked at Anders and said, no, and then he added, less abruptly, and not with a smile, or not with a smile on his lips, although perhaps with one in his eyes, it was difficult to tell, honestly it could have been the opposite of a smile, and with that peculiar expression, the cleaning guy added, what I would like is a raise.

Sixteen

Sometimes it felt like the town was a town in mourning, and the country a country in mourning, and this suited Anders, and suited Oona, coinciding as it did with their own feelings, but at other times it felt like the opposite, that something new was being born, and strangely enough this suited them too.

Not much changed in the look of the town, not at first, except for the look of the people in it, of course, but the town had taken a battering that winter, and considerable work needed to be done, and slowly a portion of that work was being done, nothing out of the ordinary, just a crew in hard hats working on a bridge, showering occasional sparks towards the river, or a bright yellow compactor rumbling as it resurfaced a road, the smell of fuel and fresh asphalt picked up and pushed along by the breeze.

Anders would be reminded of his father when he saw such things, and even more when he smelled such things, when he smelled cement or wet paint or unfinished lumber, and his memories of his father were not all pleasant, they were painful too, and while Anders thought he had done well by his father, especially at the end, he was not sure just how well he had done, and he suspected, or worried, that his father had not been sure either, had not been sure how Anders had done, and maybe that was the way it was for fathers and sons, or certain fathers and certain sons, but there was a love there too, Anders had the sense that his father did love him, and that he, Anders, did love his father, that they did not, in the final judgment, judge one another harshly, and this sense carried Anders through.

The clearing out of his childhood home was difficult for Anders, but it had to be done, and Oona helped him, and they sanded and spackled and hammered and brushed, and they would later remember these times, the two of them, semi-dressed, exposed skin dotted in paint, as among the closest of their times, and a photo Oona took of them like that, digital, but printed and mounted in physical form, was placed in the bedroom they would share, and it would later serve them as a reminder, a reminder of the start of their nesting together, whenever in the future they fought.

The house was stripped to its bones, layers of dirt and smoke and dust removed, and Anders and Oona remade the room his parents had had as their own room, and in the third bedroom, which for decades had been a home office, since no sibling of Anders's had ever arrived to lay claim to it, despite the earnest attempts and hopes of Anders's parents, they made that room into an exercise and meditation room, but they filled it as well with some of the things that had belonged to Anders's parents and that Anders wished to keep, knickknacks and pictures and a small trophy of his father's and his mother's framed degree, and so, despite its new purpose, despite its kettlebells and yoga mats and foam rollers, it felt familiar, the least transformed, of all the rooms in the entire house.

As for Anders's room, his childhood room, they left

it empty, freshly painted and unoccupied, as though a resident had just departed, or a resident was about to arrive, and whether this was done for a particular reason, as a nod to the past, or to the future, or to both, neither Anders nor Oona would, just then, have likely wanted to say.

The years went by swiftly for Anders and Oona, more and more swiftly, as they do for us all, and while memories of whiteness receded, memories of whiteness lingered too, and when their daughter was born, a tough little girl in a fragile little body, soon long and lean and quietly ferocious in her gaze, and not much of a hugger, though capable on occasion of words that were breathtakingly tender, breathtaking for being so direct and so rare, an I love you said with a solid glare in the eyes like an adult, said almost as an accusation, yes, when their daughter arrived, and grew fast, too fast, into a woman, they wanted to give her things from before, her inheritance, and they spoke of whiteness then, and what it had been, and of Anders's father, very like their daughter, utterly different but also very like her, and of

Anders's mother, the teacher, and of Oona's father, and of Oona's brother, of all of them, their daughter's ancestors, the people she flowed from, and she listened, she was open to listening, but calmly, without asking for more, and it was never clear to her parents how much she, or any of the young, truly understood.

Anders and Oona did not speak too much of the past, but Oona's mother, the girl's grandmother, did so far more, and tried to impart a sense of how it had been, of what they had really come from, of the whiteness that could no longer be seen but was still a part of them, and the girl was fond of her grandmother, and remarkably tolerant of her grandmother, and so she surprised her grandmother when she stopped her one day, when she held her grandmother's hands, and said stop, that was all, just one word, stop, and it was not much, but it affected her grandmother, deeply, because her grandmother could see, could see that the girl was embarrassed, and not embarrassed for herself, but embarrassed for her, of her, of her grandmother, and her grandmother felt a blaze of anger in that moment, but more than anger she felt loss, a potent sense of loss, but the girl did not let go of her hands, she held on to them, she held on to them and watched the emotions flaming in her grandmother's eyes, and when the emotions had flamed for a while, and were ebbing, were calmer, the girl brought her face down, and kissed the papery skin of her grandmother's knuckle, soft lips, a hint of moisture, and she waited and waited until her grandmother finally shook her head and, somehow, somehow, smiled.

Oona was close to her daughter, a closeness that waxed and waned as the child grew, but that always managed to return when Oona began most to fear for it, and Oona was constantly amazed and perplexed by her, by the hardness in her, and by her quiet confidence too, and Oona wondered if she had been like that herself when she was younger, and maybe she had been, a bit, but it was tricky to know for sure, and her daughter was small but seemed big, seemed bigger than her body, bigger than Oona, taking up space in a room even without speaking, like a gunslinger slouched alertly in the corner of a saloon.

Oona worried less for her daughter as her daughter

got older, and this was a relief to them both, as Oona had thoroughly scrutinized her daughter for signs of her brother's woundedness, and of her own woundedness, and Oona had not readily found them, or had found them only with increasing difficulty, and when they fought, Oona and her daughter, which was not often, Oona discovered she could be at once furious with her child's stubbornness and secretly pleased with the youngster's ability to stand her ground.

Anders and Oona did not have a second child, and as the years passed they made love with less regularity, at some point transitioning in their custom from nights to mornings, to those unpredictable occasions when the urge happened to come upon them both at the same time, rested and oddly potent under the sheets at the start of a new day, and on one such occasion Anders had reached out to touch Oona's back, a question, and she had smiled to herself, and moved slightly to communicate her response, and that was when the door opened and their daughter entered, as ever without a knock, but it was rare for her to be up and about early on a weekend, and rarer still for her to walk over, climb into bed, and lie between them, and she was a teenager now, and fully dressed, and she smelled of her night out, and Oona realized that her daughter had not yet gone to sleep, and she saw in her daughter's eyes not anxiety, exactly, but something else, inscrutable, and she put her arm around the girl, partly a child, who knew for how much longer, and Anders looked at her, at his daughter, and could not see her averted face, only her hair, her ear, the edges of her cheekbone and of her jaw, but also he could see her so completely, in his mind's eye, her expression, and just then he imagined her old, without wanting to, he imagined her an old woman, after he and Oona had gone, and he felt it hitting him, this image of his daughter many years hence, and he placed his brown hand on the side of her brown face, soothing her, his brown daughter, his daughter, and miraculously she let him.